Anne Manning

The lady of limited income

A tale of English country life. Vol. 2

Anne Manning

The lady of limited income
A tale of English country life. Vol. 2

ISBN/EAN: 9783337174583

Printed in Europe, USA, Canada, Australia, Japan

Cover: Foto ©Andreas Hilbeck / pixelio.de

More available books at **www.hansebooks.com**

THE
LADY OF LIMITED INCOME.

A Tale of English Country Life.

BY

THE AUTHOR OF "MARY POWELL."

"'Never her house or humble state torment her;
Less she would like, if less her God had sent her;
And when she dies, green turf and grassy tomb content her."
PHINEAS FLETCHER.—*The Purple Island.*

" Altrui vile negletta, a me sì cara,
Che non bramo tesor, nè real verga."
TASSO.—*La Gerusalemme Liberata Canto Settimo.*

IN TWO VOLUMES.
VOL. II.

LONDON:
RICHARD BENTLEY AND SON,
NEW BURLINGTON STREET.
1872.

CONTENTS OF VOL. II.

CHAPTER | PAGE
I. FLOWERS OF RHETORIC 1
II. DIVERTING VAGABONDS 26
III. UNEXPECTED PLEASURES AND PAINS . . 59
IV. MINISTERING WOMEN 88
V. STRUGGLING THROUGH 111
VI. THE ORCHIS-HUNT 138
VII. ENJOYING THEMSELVES 164
VIII. THE ENJOYMENT ENDED . . . 193
IX. MAKING BAD WORSE . . . 217
X. A PUZZLER 242
XI. ALL IN THE DAY'S WORK . . . 267
XII. BETTER FORTUNE ELSEWHERE . . . 290
XIII. GLIDING DOWN 312

THE LADY OF LIMITED INCOME.

CHAPTER I.

FLOWERS OF RHETORIC.

"Yet what can satire, whether grave or gay,
 And where are its sublimer trophies found?
 What vice has it subdued? whose heart reclaimed?"

COWPER.

MARGARET obtained no extension of her visit. She came with Mary to say good-bye to Miss Beaumorice, who could not help being amused as she observed the complex expression of her countenance.

"You look all the better, Margaret, for your country holiday," said she; "if you stayed here much longer, your town friends would say you were growing too fat."

" And yet I take a great deal more exercise here than at home," said Margaret, "but I thrive upon it. You must think henceforth that care is feeding on my damask cheek."

" What nonsense !" said Mary. " You will eat thicker slices of bread and butter than ever. It will be all pretence if you assume the *rôle* of the abstemious young lady."

" But the alumy London bread will account in a fair way for it if I do, and the sky-blue milk."

" I am afraid, Maggie, your love of Longfield is only cupboard love."

" No, that I am sure it is not," said Miss Beaumorice. " You and Mr. Brooke have made her stay so pleasant to her, that she is naturally sorry to go away."

" Yes, that is just it," said Margaret.

"I shall miss my morning run round the garden, and my nice walks here—"

"And your novel reading by the hour together," said Mary, ironically.

"Well, that has been one of my many treats," said Margaret, with frankness, "but I am going to be an intellectual young lady now, and Miss Beaumorice is going to start me off with a book in three volumes."

"That sounds wonderfully like a novel."

"But it is not one," interposed Miss Beaumorice. "I have packed it for you, Margaret; mind you let me know how you like it."

"Yes, I will indeed. And I have an object, now, in improving in drawing. When I come again I may try a little sketching. 'When will that be, say the bells of Stepney?'" with a droll look at Mary.

"Aye, when, indeed?" said Mary, "not till Miss Brooke has come and gone, and perhaps a few others.   It is just as I feared, Miss Beaumorice ! I cannot get more than a week's reprieve."

" Make the most of it, then," said Miss Beaumorice, " and try to look forward to her visit as a treat."

" John contrives to prevent that, by continually telling me she is such a piece of perfection—and he does not know her very well himself.   When he was at home she was at school, and when she left school he was at college."

" But probably they corresponded."

" Oh, but how deceptive letters are ! People always show their best side, and keep their little faults out of sight."

" Or think they do, at any rate," said Miss Beaumorice, " but habitual, characteristic thoughts are often revealed in spite of that."

" I think Alicia reveals a good deal of self-conceit.   However, I mean to be prepared for it. When are you coming to hear John preach, Miss Beaumorice? It is a shame that you have not heard him yet."

" Well, I will come over to-morrow afternoon, unless it rains ; but the fact is, I have my little duties on Sunday that prevent my wandering much from my own church."

" Oh, but to hear a friend !—a friend's husband ! If you don't come, I shall think you have taken up a prejudice against him."

" That would be quite unfounded."

" Well, I shall look on your coming as a certain thing. I am sure the weather will be fine, and you must stay to tea."

" Yes, do," said Margaret earnestly.

" I shall like it very much, weather permitting."

" Oh, I'm sure it will be fine," said both the sisters.

The weather proved all that had been prophesied—all that could be wished. It may have surprised the reader that Miss Beaumorice had not yet found an opportunity of benefitting by Mr. Brooke's ministry. But she was by no means given to change, and had, besides, an instinctive feeling that she might not relish Mr. Brooke's preaching as much as Mr. Nuneham's, or Dr. Garrow's. That misgiving was an insufficient excuse for not putting it to the test; besides, it was an attention she owed her young friends; she set forth, therefore, determined to be pleased and profited, on Sunday afternoon.

Lambscroft and Longfield have hitherto been undescribed, because, at the season when these annals began, there really was nothing very attractive in either of them. They were then in leafless, naked bareness, either frost-bound, snow-covered, or surrounded by mud and slush. But now, at the end of May, they were as pretty as could be; as *they* could be, at any rate.

Longfield church was much older and prettier than Mr. Nuneham's modern district church of St. Thaddeus. Lambscroft was altogether quite a recent place, deriving its existence from its convenient proximity to the branch railway line, which induced sanguine speculators to sow villas and cottages just where land was cheap, without any general purpose of uniformity. And though this absence of plan is one of the reasons why our English villages and hamlets are so original and attractive, Lambscroft dated its rise, not from the old times when our forefathers combined good taste and sagacity, provided for beauty as well as comfort, but from these skimp, scrimping times, when building societies and master builders take every advantage of each other within the law, with total unconcern for the incoming tenants. Consequently Miss Beaumorice, with a strong love of the picturesque, had by no means been charmed with her locality when she first settled in it, and had only become attached to it from habit. Longfield when she made its acquaintance, pleased her much more, and it was only the fact that there was no house there for her, large or small, that altogether reconciled her to being established in the adjacent hamlet. But then there were many minor disadvantages which would have been drawbacks to her at Longfield; namely, its distance from the railway, its poor array of shops, and its reputed insalubrity on account of its lying low, and being insufficiently drained. The main reason of her fondness for Lambscroft, however, was that she liked the people who lived in it.

The walk taking her rather longer than she had calculated on, she only reached the quaint old church just as the bell ceased ringing; and in spite of expressive looks from Mary and Margaret, she availed herself of a seat nearer at hand than theirs, and almost in front of the reading desk, into which the pew-opener ushered her. A hymn was heartily if not very harmoniously sung; Dr. Garrow conducted the service with a good deal of devotional fervour, reading the first lesson, Mr. Brooke reading the second. Miss Beaumorice was interested and warmed by the service. Then another hymn, and then Mr. Brooke appeared in the pulpit, his rector just under him. His very first utterance disappointed Miss Beaumorice, and as he proceeded, the feeling increased. She thought him sententious and unpractical; he raised difficulties that his congregation would never have dreamed of, to refute them with excessive sarcasm. "What good *can* the poor people derive from all this?" thought Miss Beaumorice, with chagrin; and unguardedly looking towards Mary, she found her watching her with such keen scrutiny, that she felt she must let her face tell no tales.

The effort to preserve a stolid impenetrability was tiresome and distracting; she lost the connection, and was only recovering it when a loud hem from Dr. Garrow almost made her start. She was not sure whether he had merely cleared his throat, or meant to protest against something in the sermon. Mary's sharp eyes were on her again, so that Miss Beaumorice was almost provoked with her, and altogether felt she had heard a most unsatisfactory sermon.

The catechizing that she felt sure would follow, was uncomfortable to think of; but here, Mary's complacent belief that she must have been delighted came to her aid.

"Well, how did you like him?" began she eagerly, directly they had quitted the church path and its numerous groups. "It was such a treat to watch you! I know exactly what you thought, especially about the apples of Sodom; quite a new metaphor, I think ?"

" I have heard them used in metaphors before," said Miss Beaumorice, " but the application was different."

" O yes, and that was where the point lay—the application was quite original."

" And the mirage in the desert," said Margaret, " I liked that still better; I keep a list of John's similes."

Mary smiled approvingly. " The truth is he has a very fertile imagination," said she, " and therefore deals in imagery. It comes to him as easy as possible; whereas I believe you might hunt through one of Dr. Garrow's sermons from beginning to end, without being able to find the smallest figure of speech."

" Dr. Garrow is of quite a different school," said Miss Beaumorice, smiling a little.

" Quite," said Mary, emphatically.

"A very different school, but a very good one for all that," said Miss Beaumorice.

"Oh, of course, in his old-fashioned way. I can't see him where I sit, in the chancel, but I often picture his face, while John is preaching just over him. Sometimes I fancy the good old gentleman sleeps. At any rate, he gives a loud 'hem!' now and then, as if to assure us he is awake."

Here they entered the house.

"But with regard to John,—now did not you think——oh, here he comes. John, we are talking about you; we have been talking over your sermon."

"Much obliged," said he very smilingly. "But what do you think of Dr. Garrow's hauling me over the coals?"

"No?" incredulously.

"He has though, actually. When we were in the vestry, 'My dear Brooke,' said he, in his patronizing, self-satisfied way, 'your pronunciation of Mephibosheth is no doubt the last new improvement; but, do you know, I'm an old gentleman, and like what is old, and the name has been accented the other way from time immemorial. It won't do, you know, for you and me to pull different ways; so, if you please, we'll call it my way in future. *Seniores priores;* the school-children follow my lead, and would only think you did not know how to pronounce the word.'"

"The idea!" gasped Mary. "And what did you say?"

"Say? I only bowed. I could not say anything."

"Capital!" cried Mary; "was it not, Miss Beaumorice? He did not commit himself in the least."

"Yes, I think he did the best thing he could," said Miss Beaumorice. "Dr. Garrow is so much his senior, and accustomed to be deferred to; and really with reason, for he is a most excellent man."

"Oh, of his excellence there is no dispute," said Mr. Brooke, still in high good humour; "but that does not hinder his being dreadfully benighted."

"By the way," began Miss Beaumorice, and she went off to something which hardly could be lawfully called by the way, but which opportunely diverted the dialogue into a new channel, without any apparent strangeness. Afterwards, as she went home, she thought what a narrow escape she had had of a very awkward controversy, in which she could hardly have been honest without giving pain and offence. But on the whole, her desire of sitting under Mr. Brooke's ministry, which had somehow been never very strong, was now considerably lessened; and she thought what a good thing it was to stick to one's own church, and what a privilege to have so excellent an incumbent as Mr. Nuneham.

She did not see Margaret again after

this evening; Mr. Brooke was going to London by an early train, and had engaged to take care of Margaret home. Mary had devices of her own which would keep her fully engaged, and as Miss Beaumorice knew this, she did not think it necessary to invade her solitude. It happened that a variety of small matters kept both of them engaged for a few days without any need or wish to call on the other. At the end of that time Miss Beaumorice felt impelled to look in on Mrs. Caryl. The little manuscript had been returned with a civil but decided refusal. Why was it declined? Of course she was disappointed. No reason was alleged; of course there must be one. After teazing herself with various conjectures, some of them humiliating, others absurdly wide of the mark, she bethought her of Mrs. Caryl, reported so sympathetic; and though with a strong repugnance to open the subject to her, she found she had a yet stronger incli-nation to venture on it, since it *could* do no real harm, and might lead to what was advantageous and desirable.

So Miss Beaumorice took the bold step, and reached Mrs. Caryl just at the right moment when she had cleared away her own morning's work, and taken the little walk to the post-office which always did her so much good; and was quite at leisure for any act of kindness. The conversation ranged over almost everything but the one *in petto*, and Miss Beaumorice felt she must lead to it, however awkwardly she began.

"I came to speak to you about something which——I am afraid you will think ——"

"Authorship," said Mrs. Caryl, quickly; on which they both laughed. The ice was broken successfully.

"Ah, I told you you would come about

it some day," said Mrs. Caryl, merrily, though she really had told her no such thing. "I am so glad. Well?"

"I'm afraid it is not well," said Miss Beaumorice. "I proved to be just as stupid as I thought I was at first. I wrote something slight and sent it to Messrs. Truebury, and they have declined it with thanks—no reason assigned."

"What was its nature?" said Mrs. Caryl.

"Oh, only a little magazine sketch; not a story."

"Ah, but they have such a predilection for stories. Why did you send to them in preference to any other house?"

"Really I had no particular reason, except that they have brought out many nice books."

"Harmonizing with your essay in any way?"

"Oh, no."

"If you would entrust me with it, I might very likely tell you in five or ten minutes why it would not suit them."

"I wish so you would! I don't much like your seeing it, but still——"

"You think the public at large less formidable than one solitary reader," said Mrs. Caryl, laughing.

"In theory, no ; in reality, yes ;" said Miss Beaumorice. "The public at large are out of sight and out of mind, but you are in sight and *in terrorem.*"

"Oh, yes, I know the thing completely. I have felt it often enough. Dear me, is this it? Not very long at any rate. How clearly and evenly you write! Printers like such manuscript as this. It will not take me very long to read. If you do not mind looking over that new magazine meanwhile, I will do so at once."

"Thank you very much." And Miss Beaumorice immediately followed the suggestion, and Mrs. Caryl, with her kind, thoughtful look, immediately began to read the MS. Dead silence. In about seven minutes she said quietly,—

" I like this—I like it very much,—but something strikes me already which may have hindered your success."

Miss Beaumorice was instantly all attention.

" Messrs. Truebury," pursued Mrs. Caryl, " could not possibly like this, because it is completely counter to what they have lately published in ——." And she went into details with such clearness that Miss Beaumorice at once felt their force.

" Now," continued she, " you have nothing to do but this,—to draw your pen through this paragraph from here to here, and again here, and here. And then *I* should make a fair copy of it, and therefore recommend you not to mind the trouble, especially as in all probability you will

strengthen and curtail as you do so, and
thereby wonderfully improve your article.
When it is finished, don't send it to Truebury again, but to ——. Nay, let me send
it for you, and we will hope for better luck
next time."

"How excessively kind of you!" said
Miss Beaumorice, with delight. "Like
the idle householder in ' Sam Slick,' ' I feel
quite encouraged.'"

"You're not a bit like that lazy fellow,"
said Mrs. Caryl, "and therefore it is that
I find it such a pleasure to help you. Of
course I cannot certify your success, but I
think I can predicate it. The desire to be
an author by no means indicates the ability
for it,—it often proceeds from quite unworthy motives, or from fleeting wishes,
unaccompanied by originality, or even common industry. Of what good is it for
people to cover paper without any distinct
design, by entertaining to instruct, or by in-

teresting to improve? Even where that desire exists, ignorance of what has been done, and well done already, sometimes makes writers think themselves inventing, when they are only repeating. This is only waste of time, you know, and sometimes sours as well as disappoints people. What makes me think you will or may succeed, if you give your mind to it, is that you produce *fresh thoughts*. Here now—and here,—" and she read short sentences from the essay. "These are new and terse and true, and likely to be remembered. So I think you will succeed ; or if you do not, that you deserve to do so."

Saying which, she smilingly returned the manuscript to her.

"Thank you more than I can express," said Miss Beaumorice. "You have made me see my way, and it will be my own fault if I do not follow it. Of course the question of success even then remains open; it is happy for me, therefore, that it is not one of primary importance to me, as it must be to many, and may some day be to me."

"Well, I hope not," said Mrs. Caryl, "though it is always a good thing to have two strings to one's bow; something to fall back upon in time of adversity, which authorship is to many, God being their helper. Do you remember Madame de Genlis telling Lady Morgan she had *twelve trades*, by any one of which she could get her living in time of necessity? Perhaps the good lady might have found some of them fail if put to the test, but at any rate she had *one*, and so had Lady Morgan, that answered the purpose."

"And now I will go home while all you have said is quite clear in my head," said Miss Beaumorice, rising.

"Why, it is raining quite fast," said Mrs. Caryl, going to the window. "You cannot go yet. It seems like a thunder-shower. See that poor girl in thin dress and thin boots, with a parasol the size of a daisy. She will be wet to the skin !" And with eager solicitude to draw her into shelter, Mrs. Caryl rattled against the window-pane with her thimble.

"It is Mary !" exclaimed Miss Beaumorice. "Oh, what a pity she does not hear you !"

Mary, who was on the opposite side of the road, where there were no buildings, and scarcely any trees, looked round as Miss Beaumorice spoke and as Mrs. Caryl increased the energy of her signal, but took no notice, and only quickened her pace.

"She does not hear, or she does not understand," said Mrs. Caryl, regretfully. "Dear me, how sorry I am ! She is some distance from home, and with no shelter till she gets there. Had she run across the road, we could have dried her dress at the kitchen fire, and kept her under cover till the shower was over. I hope she will not take cold, but she looks delicate. What a pretty creature she is! I am always interested in young people, married or single. She had a nice, bright, frank-looking sister with her lately, whose looks pleased me even better than her own."

"Margaret is a very nice girl," said Miss Beaumorice. "I take a kind of aunt's interest in them both, though they are not really my nieces."

"Such interests are very good for us. Well, you had better make up your mind now that this rain will not cease for a good while, and sit quietly down and re-write your article here. It will make the time fly."

"Thank you. I will do so gladly."

When the article was re-written, read aloud, and approved, the rain had quite ceased. Miss Beaumorice thankfully consigned her work to Mrs. Caryl's hands, and started homewards, caring very little that her dinner had probably been spoilt.

CHAPTER II.

DIVERTING VAGABONDS.

"Yet even these, though feigning sickness oft,
Can change their whine into a mirthful note,
When safe occasion offers."

COWPER.

A FEW rainy days ensued, which isolated the friends from one another. On the first fine morning, Miss Beaumorice called on Mary. She was shocked at her feverish worn look and altered voice.

"My dear Mary," said she, "your windpipe is affected; you ought to have advice."

"Oh, I have only caught cold," said

Mary, with an effort at unconcern. "I take colds very heavily sometimes."

"All the more need you should get rid of them. I really shall be uneasy if you do not attend to this bronchial affection."

"Quite out of the question," said Mary. "I can only keep a lozenge in my mouth. A doctor would send me to bed, where I cannot possibly be, with Alicia in the house. Besides, I don't want to run up a doctor's bill."

"It might save a heavier one, though, if you took this cold in time," said Miss Beaumorice, anxiously.

"Oh, no, I shall do very well if I'm not worried, — nothing tries me but worry," said Mary, with a quiver in her voice; "then I cough till I tear my chest to pieces."

"I am really very sorry," said Miss Beaumorice, looking at her pityingly. "I wonder Mr. Brooke does not make you take care of yourself. You caught cold on that rainy Monday, I fear. Mrs. Caryl was so sorry you did not run across. Perhaps you did not know she tried to draw your attention."

"Yes, I did; but we have never been introduced," said Mary, "so of course I was not going to her in *that* way. She rapped at the window with her thimble! So vulgar, you know."

"Well, I would have ignored that," said Miss Beaumorice, "to escape such a wetting."

"Oh, no, I did very well. Hardly that, though, to confess the truth. I was thoroughly drenched."

"We feared so. I was sure of it. She would have been so glad to shelter you. I assure you she is not vulgar."

"Oh, opinions may be different," said Mary. "However, it can't be helped now, I am booked for a bad cold; but I can't nurse it, for to-morrow we go to the inauguration of a pet sisterhood of Alicia's— a make-believe sisterhood, I should call it, if I wanted to affront her, which I don't,— and the next day to a school feast, and the day after that to a church consecration, and the day after that——"

" But, my dear Mary, you will kill yourself."

"I can't help it if I do," said Mary, beginning to cough violently, but managing to say with a flash of humour, "I must die at the stake."

And then she coughed worse than ever, till Miss Beaumorice was actually alarmed, and brought her a glass of water from the side-table. At the same time Miss Brooke entered, and though Mary attempted an introduction, her cough put it completely out of the question, or at any rate called on them to manage it for themselves ; which Miss Brooke did with a most expressive look, and Miss Beaumorice by a slight bend and smile. Miss Brooke then ministered to Mary with almost too demonstrative kindness; perfectly silent, but giving wonderful looks; raising her feet on the sofa (which Mary immediately put down again), drawing a shawl round her (which Mary speedily dropped), and from time to time establishing quite a telegraphic communication with Miss Beaumorice, who did not respond to it very readily.

While this dumb show went on, she took a rapid survey of Miss Brooke, and made her private estimate of her. Alicia seemed to be a few years older than Mary; perhaps she was six-and-twenty. Her figure was neat, her dress exceedingly becoming. It was of rich black silk, not disfigured by any " snip and snap, just like an apple-tart," which Petruchio so objected to, but that fell in beautiful folds. A row of large black beads gave her an air almost monastic ; her head was not very well shaped, but her smoothly-banded black hair was faultless ; her forehead was not broad, but flat ; her features, which at first struck one as good, were commonplace ; the mouth flat, the eyes neither fine in themselves nor with a frank expression.

"Our dear Mary has a sad cold," was her first remark, and an undeniably true one.

"Yes," said Miss Beaumorice, "and I have been trying to persuade her to take care of it."

"Oh !"—with a look which said unutterable things.

"You know I cannot, as well as I do, Alicia," said Mary.

"Ah ! yes, indeed—that is—colds will run their course. We all know what they are. We must take up our cross, and sometimes it is a *very* light one."

The look which accompanied this good remark seemed quite to rile Mary, who began hammering the sofa-pillow as if there was a stone in it, and directly Alicia had shaken it up she tossed it away altogether.   Another telegraphic appeal to Miss Beaumorice made that kind lady feel that she was being made a kind of tool of against Mary, and that it was not altogether pleasant or safe to be an involuntary umpire respecting every trivial matter. So she began about the weather, generally a safe subject, and observed she hoped it was going to be fine, as the barometer was rising.   Miss Brooke said, with intense interest,—

"You *have* one?"

"Oh, no," said Miss Beaumorice, "Mr. Nuneham has one in his hall."

"Mr. Nuneham is the incumbent, I believe, of St. Thaddeus?"

"Yes."

"Ah! a very holy man, I daresay."

"He does not account himself so, certainly. A very humble man, all who know him must admit. A very devotional, self-denying, earnest, benevolent man—always thinking of others."

"Why, then, he *must* be a holy man," said Miss Brooke, plaintively.

"Yes, I think we may account him so, if it is a word to apply to any one."

"Oh, *surely* it is. I'm sure I hope so. I should be miserable indeed if I did not."

Miss Beaumorice thought it would be safest to shun polemics, and therefore returned to the weather.

"I hope it will be dry to-morrow," said she, "for I suppose you have a long drive before you."

"Yes, Alicia is going to treat us to a fly," said Mary, stifling her cough. "So kind !"

Alicia raised her hand in deprecation. "'Tis nothing." said she to Miss Beaumorice. "Dearest Mary makes too much of it. I wish she had not mentioned the fact. We should—

"'Do good by stealth, and blush to find it fame.'"

Mary was here seized with such an uncontrollable desire to laugh, that it brought on her cough with frightful violence. Alicia looked frightened rather than concerned, and Mary herself shed a few tears from downright weakness. She leant her head against Miss Beaumorice's shoulder; and just then Mr. Brooke came in, and looked surprised and grieved.

"Why, Mary, what's the matter?" said he, very kindly.

"She has coughed to exhaustion," said his sister.

"Poor thing! poor thing!" said he, sitting down beside her, and putting his arm round her. Mary was comforted, and looked up at him with eyes full of tears, but a smile on her lips.

" I'm better now," she said in a low voice.

He kissed her and held her hand, and his kind looks and words had the happiest effect on poor Mary. Miss Beaumorice liked him better than she had ever done before. Miss Brooke gave her a look which seemed to say, " How touching !"

" Mary has evidently a very serious cold," said Miss Beaumorice to Mr. Brooke in her most matter-of-fact, though kindly way; " and as she tells me she has several en-gagements coming on, I think it will be the wisest way for her to go to bed at once, and nurse herself for them. I am sure I shall be upheld by you admirable nurses."

" In broad daylight ?" began Mary.

Miss Beaumorice rejoined cheerfully—

" Yes, in broad daylight, my dear girl,

and I shall expect when I come here again, to find you ever so much better. Mr. Brooke and Miss Brooke will be excellent companions, and must have plenty to say to each other; and as for you, you shall have a good novel and plenty of nice cooling drinks; and I know you of old, Mary, so don't pretend that you will dislike that."

Mary could not help smiling; and, in short, Miss Beaumorice carried her point, and actually saw her into her bed-room, helped her to undress, and tucked her in, "Not for the first time," as she cheerfully remarked. Then supplying her with a book from a book-box which had just arrived, she gave her a kiss, consigned her to warmth and solitude, and made her own way home without longer delay.

She thought with pain of many sad cases of neglected colds, and wished Mr. Brooke would see that advice was necessary, and authority, too ; for where is the good of the best advice without authority to enforce it on the patient's companions as well as on the patient ? How is a sickly mother, for instance, to get a week's quiet and change if her family won't spare her ? How is an overworked brain to rest if an overworked head of a household cannot obtain it ?

When Miss Beaumorice reached home she found the Nunehams had sent her some beautiful strawberries, nestling in dark green leaves. She passed these on to Mary at once, with a loving message.

The next day was bright, but with a dry, cutting wind, worse for Mary than rain. She thought of her many times, and feared she had gone in the fly. Somehow Miss Brooke did not give her the idea of one who would bate one jot of consideration, however ready to perform little offices, and to speak of bearing little crosses. Miss Beaumorice thought she might venture to call on Mary, even though she had an engagement.

To her great pleasure Mary was at home, and the others had gone without her. Mary was in bed, looking dreadfully feverish; and she stretched out her arms to Miss Beaumorice with a little cry of joy.

"So good of you to come," she said, coughing; "I was persuaded you would, and yet not quite sure, so I am doubly glad. I made them think I was quite sure, or they would have stayed—at least Alicia would—and that would have been dreadful."

"You must not talk, my dear Mary—I must talk for both. I don't think she would have given up the engagement. It would have been such a disappointment to others as well as herself. I thought of you many times yesterday. Your husband would not have gone without you, and no doubt they would both be missed."

" Oh, yes, the superior, as they call her,

quite reckoned on them, so it would not have done not to go. Dear Miss Beaumorice, she's no more a superior than you or I ; they take no vows, unless of their own making, and silly enough some of them are. Hurtful, too—" coughing.

" I dare say ; but now you must be quiet a little while."

" No, no," said Mary, feverishly, " I shall explode like a soda water bottle if I do, for I have pent up so many things to tell you, that I shall die if you don't hear them out. One of their vows, at least of Alicia's, is fasting."

" I believe," suggested Miss Beaumorice, " fish is very wholesome twice a week."

" But she eats *nothing*—absolutely nothing till dinner," insisted Mary, coughing violently, " and you may imagine how hungry she then is."

" Nothing ? Oh, that must be a *façon de parler*—dry bread, perhaps."

"Nothing at all—not so much as a lozenge! John laughed and spoke of the ancient Britons subsisting for days on a bean, up to their necks in water."

"Miss Brooke could not equal that."

"No, but she said how fine it was, and what a pity such self-denial had not been sanctified by a holy motive. Miss Beaumorice, she will sicken me of the word holy, if she goes on so," said Mary excitedly; "I think she is making me wicked—I quite dread her influence; it is so unwholesome to me. She comes into the room without noise, with that emblazoned prayer-book of hers, sits down without invitation, and begins without a word of preface, in such a dreadful sing-song—'plain tune' they call it, that I really do not know whether it is about the Queen's accession or gunpowder plot."

"Mary, you are highly feverish, or you would not be so amusing; I must give you a sedative, my dear, unless you will quiet yourself a little; I shall not stop, if I find you cannot help talking to me."

This silenced Mary for a minute.

"The Queen's accession service," continued Miss Beaumorice, "is very beautiful; and I only regret its now being seldom or never used. Considering what a good Queen we have, we might all use it heartily; and it would fan our loyalty, and bring down a blessing on the land, and on the dear Queen herself."

"I know you are very loyal," said Mary, softly.

"Yes, I am," said Miss Beaumorice; "considering all we have suffered from bad kings, and how few comparatively have been the good ones, I think it a special blessing that we live in the reign of a good, pure-minded, high-minded Queen, who sets us so praiseworthy an example. So long a reign, too! and may it be yet longer! as long as it is good for her and for us that she should be here."

Mary was toned down by this, and after a little pause, she said more quietly, "you must not think that I have really taken a dislike to the prayer-book, because I dislike Alicia's particular one. I value it very much, and I remember you, dear Miss Beaumorice, reading to me from it once, when I was very ill and feverish with the measles. Do you ?"

"Perfectly. I read you the twenty-third psalm."

"Would you mind reading it to me again."

"Not at all. I shall like to do so very much."

And so she read it in a gentle, calming voice, while Mary's face gradually lost its harassed look. After a short silence she said—

"That is reading I like. I like it even

better than John's. Alicia bores me with her inopportune passages at inopportune times, and her way of reading is most lugubrious. She makes the hundred and third psalm as dismal as if it were one of the seven penitential ones. That can't be right, you know."

"Your cough is rather quieter, now, Mary; and here comes a nice cup of arrow-root for you."

"Ah, I was beginning to want something to allay this irritation. Thank you, Susan; you have made it very nicely. And thank *you*, dear Miss Beaumorice, for those beautiful strawberries; John and Alicia ate them all but five."

"I meant them for you," said Miss Beaumorice, annoyed.

"Yes, I know; and I ate five and enjoyed them immensely, and sent the rest down to them, saying I had had enough."

"That was very nice of you, Mary."

"I have not done good by stealth, and blushed to find it fame," said Mary, laughing, and then coughing.

"Now, Mary, your *rôle* must be that of the Princess Hold-your-tongue, unless you want me to go home."

"Oh, please don't! pray don't! I want you to dine here. I told John you would."

"Well, you must obey orders then."

"Yes, yes. Susan is dressing you a nice lamb chop; and some of the peas you so kindly sent us. She will bring up the tray at one. Now do take off your bonnet and shawl, and sit down by me again, or you will make me cough."

"That is a very cunning threat of yours. I have no objection to stay if you will be good. This is a bright day, but with a cold wind. It will suit Mr. and Miss Brooke very well, though it would not have suited you."

"Oh, they will enjoy it," said Mary. "I

am glad for their sakes it is fine, instead of raining as it did on that unfortunate Monday. How wet I was, to be sure! I had gone to bespeak some fish for Wednesday, for you know how difficult it is to get any, and Alicia ignores impracticabilities" (coughing again.)

"Well, now it is my turn to talk. I hope Margaret reached home safely. How happy you made her; she did not like going at all."

"No, I don't think she did; and I'm sure I miss her very much, but you know she could not be here always. She had to make way for others. Turn and turn about, especially the first year."

"Yes. I daresay visits will be the fashion this summer, and freedom from them the next."

"Well, I don't know what to say to that; perhaps, and perhaps not. Alicia knows nothing, practically, about housekeeping, and one of her fixed ideas is that *everybody*, without reference to small means and small families, should make soup for the poor, when perhaps they have as much as they can do not to show they are poor themselves. Of course, wealthy people like the Garrows, can have coppers full of soup, without stinting for plenty of gravy-beef and vegetables ; and as I tell Alicia, every poor person may go there on soup days and have pitchers-full of soup fit for an alderman. But too much of a good thing is good for nothing, and I have reason to know that Mrs. Garrow's soup kitchen is so open to all comers, that it makes them actually dainty. At all events, there is no want of another ; and I would not have one if there were. However, Alicia,——"

Another fit of coughing, but she would go on.

"—Has already rummaged up two or three wretched Irish ; regular tramps, and

Roman Catholics besides, whom she says nobody will attend to; and therefore she insists on having these filthy people to our back door, and ten to one they will some day go off with the spoons."

Here Susan came to announce that dinner was ready, to Miss Beaumorice's relief, for she thought Mary had already talked more than enough; but she *would* have one word more, in an energetic undertone.

"So she has begged me to give her everything useless, and I am sorry to say many a scrap and slice that might be turned to account in the family, comes under that category with her. She is never out of the kitchen in the morning, while Susan is dusting the bedrooms, which is particularly inconvenient to me, and to Susan too."

"Of course. My dear Mary, may I send you a little morsel?"

"Not any, thank you; I have not the least appetite; I can touch nothing but slops. Now do you go down and make a comfortable dinner."

"Shall I leave you a book?"

"Yes, please; but perhaps I shall go to sleep. She said on Saturday, 'this mutton is beginning to taint—I'm sure it may go into the stew'—when it was quite good! and was to have made out the servants' dinner."

Miss Beaumorice thought it best to reply only by a silent look, and went down to her dinner, which for politic reasons she did not hurry over. When she went up again, after looking over the *Times*, she was very glad to find Mary asleep. She sat quietly beside her for some time without so much as rustling the leaves of a book, and was much concerned to notice her short breathing and general look of indisposition.

Mary woke refreshed, however, and happily Miss Beaumorice was able to lead the conversation quite away from Miss Brooke's imperfections. Leaving her, at length, tolerably comfortable, and seemingly inclined for another nap before the absentees' return; she consigned her to Susan's quiet attention, and returned home about her usual tea hour.

On the way, she met Mrs. Garrow, who came up to her and said,—

"Good afternoon, Miss Beaumorice; pray can you tell me how Mrs. Brooke is? I have not seen her anywhere lately, and on Sunday she seemed to have a bad cold."

"Yes. She is nursing it in bed to-day," said Miss Beaumorice, "while Mr. Brooke and his sister are keeping an engagement without her. I have been sitting with her, and trying to persuade her to have advice, which she is disinclined to. She is very poorly indeed, though."

"How sorry I am. She ought to see Mr. Finch, for I don't suppose she knows how to manage herself." And then ensued some details which increased Mrs. Garrow's motherly concern for Mary.

"I am often vexed with her, poor thing," she said, "because she dresses too airily, and seems to have no notion of prudence. I was on my way to her now, to scold her a little; however, she is spared that, since you have told me how ill she is. She ought to have good nursing from Mr. Brooke's sister, but somehow that young lady does not give me the idea of a good nurse; and, dear me! how she goes on in church! *Such* genuflexions!"

She looked sharply at Miss Beaumorice as she spoke, to see whether she was on dangerous ground; but after a pause went on.

"Nothing annoys me more in church than for some one who audibly makes the responses, to do so about half a minute after everybody else. They ought to keep time if they repeat them at all; at any rate if audibly. Don't you think so ?"

" Yes, I quite agree with you," said Miss Beaumorice.

" Oh, it's tormenting. Worse than not keeping step with the person you walk with—much worse than that; because it seems sanctimonious, and meant to draw attention. Tablets, too."

This was general observation, without application.

" And really, one need hardly book one's own brother," continued Mrs. Garrow, approaching personality; " I should think he would lend her his sermon at home if she asked him." Then abruptly changing the subject,—

" I have a bone to pick with Mrs. Brooke when she gets better, about encouraging a worthless set of Irish tramps,

who are harbouring here for the haying, or
for anything that may turn up. The *real*
haymakers I am never hard upon; indeed
I am kind to them; but these are quite of
another stamp — they have been at the
races, and are now sleeping under hedges
and living by their wits—by no means
safe customers. They would soon have
been cleared out of the parish, but Mrs.
Brooke seems to have taken them in
hand."

"Pardon me, Miss Brooke," interrupted
Miss Beaumorice.

"Oh, is it so? Well, that seems much
more natural; for in fact, Mrs. Brooke is by
no means too fond of poor people—even
decent poor, whom I want her to like, and
who deserve all the relief she can afford
them. Miss Brooke—ah, that explains,—
that coincides with my idea of her; though
why *she* should feel called to take them
up, or what business it is of hers to make

soup in another lady's house ? Humph ! What was it I heard about a sisterhood ? Does she belong to one ?"

" No, I think not; only interested in one."

" Ah, that may lead to the other. I am old-fashioned enough, Miss Beaumorice, to be thankful to Ridley and Latimer, and to Baxter and Hammond and Jackson for the sound doctrine divested of puerilities they bequeathed to us. I have no mind for us to play away our privileges. They cost our forefathers too dear. Is that your feeling ?"

" Yes, quite," said Miss Beaumorice.

" Ah, I thought it was. I fancy you and I are much of a mind about a good many things. I hope the Brookes may be influenced by you. But, dear me, our pretty little friend was hardly cut for a curate's wife, and would never have inclined to be one, I suppose, if a nice young clergyman had not happened to make her an offer.

Girls should not drift into it; it's a vocation."

"Mary had no opportunity of studying
it in her London home.   Her disposition is
very——"

"Yes, yes, she would have repaid training, if it had been afforded her in time; it
now comes rather late.   However, she is
but young yet.   And the danger is of her
taking the wrong sort of training,—of fan-
cying because Miss Brooke is pretty, and
prettily dressed, that all those bowings and
bendings and drawlings and intonings are
as good as if they were in Holy Writ.   *I*
call it will-worship.   What in the world
made poor young Mr. Brooke talk about
Mephi Bosheth the other day?   My dear
Miss Beaumorice, I thought I must have
laughed.   I was quite in terror at being
so near it.   I saw my daughter bite her
lips.   What must the school children have
thought?   I don't pretend to be a linguist,

but Dr. Garrow is one, and my grandfather was a D.D., and I have been in pretty many of our cathedrals and churches, and I never heard the stress laid on the third syllable yet."

"Young men are attracted by anything new," began Miss Beaumorice.

"New? but this was an Old Testament name. Our pronunciation may not be that of the ancient Hebrews, but it is that of Colet, and Linacre, and More, and Erasmus, and all our early reformers, so I think it is good enough for *us*. Just look!" cried Mrs. Garrow, as they came to a turn in the road, over-arched by fine elms in their early green.

A stout, healthy girl of about twelve, bare-footed, ragged, and with a heavy baby at her back, was having a game of ball with a younger boy, also bare-footed and ragged —the ball was—a half-quartern loaf!

Quick as light the boy saw them, and

did not return the ball. The girl, whose back was to them, turned round and straightway began begging in a professional whine.

"Please to give us a halfpenny, lady, to buy us a morsel of bread!"

"Your baby does not want bread, at any rate," said Mrs. Garrow. "He is a fine, well-fed child."

"An't he a beauty, my lady? sure an' your heart will be soft to him? Please give us a penny, my lady!"

"You yourself don't look much out of condition. How came your cheeks to be so round and red?"

"He that feeds the sparrows, my lady—"

"Hush! hush! no profanity! You are trying to deceive me. You are not in want."

"May ye never know what want is, my lady. Sure ye look as if ye could spare a penny."

" Who gave you your last meal ?"

" A fine young lady that's the curate's sister, my lady—glory be her rest! *She'll* never want the poor girl's blessing."

" Did she give you the loaf you were playing ball with ?"

The girl's eyelids involuntarily twinkled.

" Sure an' she did, my lady; and we wouldn't eat a morsel of it, but were carrying it straight to my mother."

" Well, I hope that's true, at any rate ; though it did not seem as if you were in a hurry to reach her."

" Sure, my lady, we were so glad to get it for her, that we couldn't help larking a little."

" You're a sad set of deceivers, I'm afraid. If I give a penny to the baby, not to you, (his cheeks are no deceivers, at all events) what will you say then ?"

" Sure an' I'll pray for ye, my lady."

" Pray ? but to whom ?" said Mrs. Garrow, putting a penny into the hand of the fine little fellow, who immediately tried to put it into his mouth.

"To the mother of God, my lady."

"Fie, fie,—she will never hear you. It is not your fault that you have been badly taught; but the Virgin Mary is not the answerer of prayer. She herself, good and blessed woman as she was, said to the Jews of her Son, 'Whatsoever He saith unto you, do it.' And though that only referred to a particular case, it literally applies to all. He desired us to ask everything of the Father in His name, He said nothing about His mother—You are not attending to me—Go, go, take your mother her loaf!"

And off they ran; the boy turning re-peated somersaults along the dusty road, and then re-producing the loaf and playing ball with it.

CHAPTER III.

UNEXPECTED PLEASURES AND PAINS.

Have you no words? Oh, think again !
Words flow apace when you complain,
And fill a friend's unwilling ear
With the sad tale of all you fear.

THE evening post brought Miss Beaumorice an unexpected treat —a double column proof of her essay ! She could hardly believe her eyes, and was delighted that a rainy evening gave her the promise of uninterrupted enjoyment of it. "How nice it looks !" thought she ; and then felt ashamed of herself for the vanity of the feeling, till it occurred to her that no woman minds taking credit to herself for the happily devised trimming of a dress, or clever disposition of her furniture, or the arrangement of a nosegay, or the laying out a garden : no, nor is she accused of conceit by her neighbours or her family, for calling their attention to such achievements, by saying, "See what I have done ! is it not pretty ?" Miss Beaumorice told herself there was no difference, and yet she felt there was one. She felt she could fearlessly call attention to her clever bonnet-trimming or pretty nosegay, but would be penetrated with shame at the smallest suspicion of being proud of her little essay. Why was this ? She did not know, nor trouble herself much to find out ; but luxuriously nestling in her favourite seat, enjoyed reading the proof, first rapidly, then deliberately ; then twice more with the utmost care to detect and correct the smallest error.

"I owe this pleasure to dear Mrs. Caryl," thought she. "I will go to tell her of it in the morning."

But the morning's post brought her a rather anxious letter from Margaret, saying they could not make out how Mary was, whether really ill or only with a troublesome cold that would soon have run its course: and begging to know Miss Beaumorice's real opinion of it.

Miss Beaumorice thought she had better see Mary again before writing, as there was a chance she might be better. Unfortunately she found poor Mary not better, but worse, in a high state of nervous depression, and so hoarse that her voice was hardly audible. But first she saw Alicia Brooke in the drawing-room, busily engaged in copying an illuminated page from some old missal, of a female saint or worthy, somewhat in the Chinese style of art, wholly out of drawing, and with an expression that by no means made amends for it.

"Very sweet, isn't it ?" said Alicia, pensively, as she looked at Miss Beaumorice and then at the painting.

"The colours are very vivid," said Miss Beaumorice, after a little pause.

"Ah, yes—and after so many hundred years ! We have no such colours now—nor yet such painters."

"Surely we have made a little progress in art since the Heptarchy ?"

"It depends on what style of art you are thinking of. This is sacred art, you know."

Here Susan came in and said her mistress would be glad to see Miss Beaumorice, so the permission was gladly acted on. She found Mary in bed.

"My dear Mary, I hoped to find you a little better to-day."

"Oh, I am very ill," said Mary, almost

in a whisper, and with tears stealing down her face. "I tried to get up, but it was no use. John saw it was not, and begged me to remain in bed."

"He was quite right. Do you feel in pain ?"

"All over, I think. I can't talk much, even to you."

"No, no."

"I just like to see you, that's all."

"My dear girl, you must not cry. You will soon be better, with only a little care ; and you must not mind that, for Mr. Brooke's sake."

"No ; only—"

She shut her eyes, but the tears oozed through them.

"I'm very weak. And he does not know how weak. He does not know what to make of it. It is so trying to hear them talking and laughing down-stairs. The walls are very thin."

"It *is* trying."

She held Mary's hot tremulous hand in hers for some time, in silence.

"What did you say?" she presently asked, as Mary's lips moved.

"How nice and cool your hand is. It is so pleasant to see a friend."

"It is very pleasant to me to know that you think me one. We have known each other a long while."

"A long while." Silence again.

"Is Alicia gone out?"

"No, she is in the drawing-room, painting."

"I wish she were out. Her presence worries me."

"That is because you are weak and feverish, my dear Mary."

"I know it, but that does not hinder it." (Then very low). "She weans John from me."

"Oh, no, my dear girl!"

" She does indeed. She is always making me appear in the wrong—making me seem worldly — he thinks her ever so much better than me—all on her own show-ing."

" It may seem so to you ; but rely on it you are mistaken."

" I cannot. She has such opportuni-ties."

" Why, Mary, I do believe you are a little jealous ; and without the least founda-tion. Make yourself quite easy ; this is only a feverish little dream. I have had such myself, and know how wretched they make one while they last ; and all at once the dream is dispelled, like a cloud by the sun shining through it—just as it is doing now !"

Mary looked wearily towards the sun-lit window and said sadly,—

" Oh, that it may be so !"

" It will, you may depend. And now,

suppose you take a little refreshment, and then let me read you to sleep."

" I could not touch a morsel of breakfast. Susan took in half a pint of milk to make me a little pudding, and Alicia has used it for those Irish."

" Provoking !" said Miss Beaumorice. " Charity begins at home. See ! here comes Susan with something nice."

Susan came in with a small mould of beautiful clear calf's foot jelly from Mrs. Garrow. Mary could not help faintly smiling.

" Now you must take a few spoonfuls of this at once," said Miss Beaumorice. "Shall I feed you ?"

" No, thank you. I can manage it."

" Now, Susan, attend, please, to my strict injunction. Let nobody have this jelly but Mrs. Brooke ; or Mrs. Garrow will be much displeased. Mind ! I shall tell her."

Susan smiled, and promised obedience. "Nobody else need see it," said she.

"Certainly not; and Mrs. Brooke is so generous that she gives things away meant expressly for herself; and it vexes people. I know it was so about the strawberries."

Susan smiled again, and Mary could not help smiling too. Meanwhile Miss Beaumorice was secretly pleased to see spoonful after spoonful slipping "down the red lane," till a competent portion had disappeared; for Mrs. Garrow was very famous for her jelly, and Mary happened to be particularly fond of it.

"Now, that will do you good," said Miss Beaumorice, with satisfaction, as Susan carried off the remainder in the basket with a lid, in which it had been sent.

"It really has revived me," said Mary. "I think there must be a good deal of wine in it."

"Depend on it, there is only just the proper proportion of everything. One would like to have the power to make such beautiful jelly as that. I can make tolerable jelly myself, but not equal to Mrs. Garrow's. You and I must ask her for her secret some day. Now I will shake up your pillow, and then read you something amusing."

"Read me another psalm, please."

"Yes, my love."

Having done which she kissed her ; and then took up a book of essays and read to herself. Presently she had the satisfaction of seeing Mary fall asleep, and then she quietly went out of the room, and out of the house : Susan opened the door for her without the least noise.

Arrived at home, Miss Beaumorice wrote to Margaret ; and then, with feelings much sobered, she went again over her proof and packed it for the printer. It was too late now, and she was too tired, to go to Mrs. Caryl.

Next morning, however, she was preparing to do so when Margaret suddenly entered. She said,—

"Oh, Miss Beaumorice, I dare say you are surprised; but—" and began to cry a little.

"I am as glad as I am surprised—nay, much more so."

"Why, you see, your letter frightened us a little ; and me a great deal—and papa said Mary ought to have advice, and wanted mamma to come down ; but mamma could not, because she had an engagement ; and I begged I might come down with a day-ticket, till papa said I might. Mamma did not like my running about the country by myself, but papa said it was all nonsense."

"And you have come down quite safely," said Miss Beaumorice, "and though Mary cannot take you in, now that Miss Brooke has her only spare bed, yet I can, with pleasure."

"Thank you very much. I should so like it! But you see I have a return-ticket, and papa and mamma expect me back."

"Then you had better go, of course, unless there is some unforeseen reason why Mary cannot spare you. They will want you to return and tell them how Mary is; but if she should very much wish for you, you have only to come down to-morrow, and be with her by day and with me at night."

"Thank you—I shall so gladly do so, if Mary wants me. How is she? Do you know?"

"I have not seen her since I wrote to you yesterday. I was thinking of going over in the afternoon, but now I shall let you go instead, and hear what you say of her on your return."

"Then now I will go," said Margaret, rising.

"As soon as you have had something to eat."

"Thank you—it does not signify. Perhaps you will let me have a slice of bread-and-butter."

"Certainly, and I will have some too."

While they ate their lunch, Miss Beaumorice told Margaret all that she thought she would like to know of Mary's case, but spoke cheerfully and hopefully, so that Margaret lost her harassed look.

"I shall be so glad if she is better, to-day!" she said. "I travelled from Charing Cross with some one who knew you, Miss Beaumorice. It was so odd to hear you spoken of, by some one I did not know. I thought he might not like it if he found out I knew you ; but I could not tell him, because mamma says we should not speak to people in railway trains."

"Who could he be, I wonder ?"

"He was a young officer, I fancy, on day leave.   He was going down to Hythe."

"Oh, it must have been Alured Ward !"

" Perhaps so, but his companion did not address him by name.   He said to him, 'The first time I came down here was to see Miss Beaumorice.' "

" Did he come on to Lambscroft ?"

" No, I changed carriages at the junction ; but he went on."

" Of course he would."

" And he said you had been very kind to him when he was ill ; quite a mother to him."

" Dear fellow !"   And Miss Beaumorice went into the details of Alured's illness ; after which she started Margaret on her way and then proceeded to execute one or two little errands. On her way she met Mr. Finch, who drew up his chaise to speak to her, and said,—

"Your friend Mrs. Caryl is very ill. Can you manage to look in on her?"

"Certainly. I will do so directly. I was on my way to her, though I did not know she was ill. A bad cold?"

"Something worse than that, though cold may have brought it on. A disease of long standing, I fancy."

"Any particular directions?"

"Nourishment, and quiet, and keeping her mind easy. I believe that is all you can do."

He waved his hand and drove off, and Miss Beaumorice proceeded on her way, full of concern; her anxiety about Mary made secondary to this new source of interest. Passing her butcher's, she desired him to send in two pounds of lean rumpsteak directly, with orders to her cook to prepare it immediately for beef jelly.

Arrived at Mrs. Caryl's, she saw at once by the servant's face that there was trouble in the house.

"Mistress is very ill, ma'am," she began.

"Yes, I know," answered Miss Beaumorice, quietly. "I met Mr. Finch, and he told me to see her."

Another moment and she was in the parlour, where poor Mrs. Caryl lay on the sofa in a disconsolate condition. Old ladies depend a good deal on their make-up. She was generally the pattern of neatness, and wore nothing but what was appropriate; but on the present occasion, a sudden faintness, followed by violent shivering, had made her powerless to help herself; and Hester, scared at her seizure, and having neither experience nor presence of mind, had heaped on her all kinds of unsuitable wraps—a rainbow-*couvre-pied*, a striped anti-macassar, a red table-cover, &c., so that in her extreme weakness and pallor, she looked bedizened like a mountebank, and, to finish all, had her cap knocked on one side. But nothing could draw Miss Beaumorice's attention from the main point, — the sad condition of her friend, whose face wore an ashy hue that she knew too well.

Mrs. Caryl opening her eyes without raising her head or moving her position in the least, said gently,—

"This is kind. I knew you would come if you heard I was ill."

"And I was already on my way to you, when I met Mr. Finch, though I did not then know how unfit you were to be alone."

"As to alone," replied Mrs. Caryl, after a short pause, returning Miss Beaumorice's affectionate pressure of the hand; "you know what Miss Maurice says in 'Sickness, its Trials and its Blessings'—that every one knows he must *die* alone, but few realize that they must, to a great extent, *live* and *suffer* alone. I have had to do so for a long time—it is no new lesson." And a tear strayed down her cheek.

"But now you require somebody," said Miss Beaumorice, tenderly.

"I won't say I require any one,—that is, but my servant,—but I certainly feel comforted by being looked in on by you."

"And I will come and stay with you a little while, if you will let me."

"No, no; I don't need that. Your own experience will tell you there must be a preparation even for one like you, so that it would add to trouble rather than lessen it. A visit from you, when convenient, just to see how I do, and to cheer me up, and to let Hester see I am not wholly deserted—"

"But at night?"

" Oh, at night I shall do very well. In the first place, I generally sleep like a baby, and when I lie awake, my thoughts are calm and comfortable.   I am used to these attacks."

" But you may want something."

" I generally have something within reach.   Always a bell; which, happily, I seldom need to ring."

" Your head is not very comfortable."

" No, the pillow has slipped—thank you. —Please take away all these strange wraps Hester has heaped on me."

" Shall I get you anything to supply their place ?"

" If you would not mind going into the room overhead, you will see my black shawl on the bed."

Miss Beaumorice speedily made a great improvement in Mrs. Caryl's comfort and appearance; not forgetting the cap; of which Mrs. Caryl was quite sensible.

"There, now you look like your usual self," said she, cheerily.

"I don't feel like my usual self, though," said Mrs. Caryl. "I am shaken all over by my fall; and my head aches badly. 'All in the day's work,'—and *my* day's work is stopped pretty effectually."

Her face saddened.

"Checked, not stopped," said Miss Beaumorice. "Checked perhaps for a day or two. And, do you know, you did *me* a good day's work. I have had a proof of my little essay."

"Oh, I am so glad. Did it look nice?"

"Yes,—so its partial mother thought. Have you any proofs of your own that you want posted?"

"Yes, there is one on the table that I shall be much obliged by your directing and posting."

"Is there any one to whom you wish a letter written about your illness?"

"Not to-day, I think—to-morrow, perhaps," said Mrs. Caryl, wistfully. "I have a very dear niece, Edith Caryl, who likes to know how I am going on; but she is at Bagnères de Bigorre now, with her invalid father. You will see a letter directed to her on the table. That will supply you with her address in case it should be wanted."

Mrs. Caryl closed her eyes, and seemed suffering.

"I hope to send good news to her if I send any," said Miss Beaumorice. "As you say, we will wait."

"Yes, that is what I have been doing a long while; many years. It does not bring death any sooner. It will come at last, whether we wait for it or not."

"Yes, to all." And after a moment's pause, she gently repeated,—

"'When gathering clouds around I view,
    And days are dark, and friends are few,

> On Him I lean, who not in vain
> Experienced every human pain.
> He knows my doubts, allays my fears,
> And counts and treasures up my tears.' "

"Do go on with it," said Mrs. Caryl, squeezing her hand, still with her eyes closed. "It is such true comfort. It is easy to feel you have often ministered to others."

"I have indeed." And she repeated the rest of the hymn. Presently she asked the prosaic question,—

"What are you going to have for dinner?"

"Mr. Finch said I might have fish, but I fear the fishmonger has not called."

"Hester can go to him while I am here."

Mrs. Caryl thankfully agreed to her doing so; and Hester was quickly despatched for a sole or a whiting. Meanwhile Miss Beaumorice made a little arrowroot, more nicely, Mrs. Caryl thought, than any she had ever tasted.

"This illness will be valuable to me," said she, thankfully, "if only for showing me what a kind, efficient nurse you are."

"You are so easy to nurse," said Miss Beaumorice. "You have no fever. My poor little friend, Mrs. Brooke, is laid up with bronchitis, and is made so much worse by feverish irritation. She cannot help it, poor thing!"

"Oh, no, it is quite involuntary sometimes, especially with the young. It makes illness much harder to bear. I pity them so for it. I think we are not half concerned enough for the sorrows of the young. They take grief and pain so heavily. Did Mrs. Brooke take cold in that rain-storm?"

"Yes."

"There is Hester. I am sorry to trouble you."

Hester brought two nice whitings, just fit for an invalid. Miss Beaumorice renewed the quiet dialogue at intervals, when she thought Mrs. Caryl could bear it.

"I am glad to hear you have a niece."

"She is such a nice creature. I had charge of her for many years. She is almost a daughter to me. Her father was obliged to retire from business rather abruptly on account of his health, before he had realized more than a moderate competence, on which they can very well live abroad. He was ordered to try the foreign baths. The firm has since got into difficulties, so it was a good thing he left it when he did. Edith writes me such entertaining letters. Sympathetic ones, too, when I need them."

"Her correspondence must be a great treat to you."

"Yes, and so are the letters of one or two old literary friends, wholly on literature, and one or two old friends to whom literature is nothing. Two or three young cadets, too—I owed them to my husband. They write to me as if I were their aunt, dear boys."

"You have many strings to tie you to life still."

"They are loose, very loose and frail. I am reconciled to that—thankful and hopeful on the whole—though the last wrench may give a little thrill."

"Our Saviour will be with you when that comes."

"I humbly trust He will."

When Miss Beaumorice at length took leave of her, Mrs. Caryl requested rather anxiously that she would be with her the next day when Mr. Finch repeated his visit, which she promised. She then left her with such little appliances about her as her state required, in a calm and patient frame of mind, with books of devotion at hand when she felt able and inclined to use them.

Margaret did not return very late, as she had been particularly desired to travel by an early evening train. She had therefore just time for a five o'clock tea with Miss Beaumorice first.

"How ill Mary is!" said she, very seriously. "Mr. Finch has seen her, and says he should have been sent for before. He says we need not be alarmed, but that she requires the utmost care."

"I am sure she does."

"John is frightened now, but Mary seems calmer now she is in Mr. Finch's hands. Miss Brooke—oh, Miss Beaumorice, how abominable she is!"

"That is rather a strong word. I think we had better let Miss Brooke alone, and not trouble ourselves with her peculiarities."

"But how can people help it in the house

with her ? Have you seen her in her sheep's clothing ?"

" What do you mean ?"

" Mary says she wore a very nice silk dress at first, but now she wears a long, straight, scanty black flannel dress, with scarcely any fulness in it, that she can hardly step out in; and Mary calls it sheep's clothing."

" Mary says very droll things sometimes, especially now she is feverish; but do you know, I think we had better not pass that on. In the first place, it is never right to use Scriptural expressions lightly; and then, again, things are apt to get altered and enlarged by other people who pick them up. If you repeat that at home, very likely one of the boys will say to somebody, ' Do you know Mary has a visitor whom she calls a wolf in sheep's clothing !' "

" Yes, that is as likely as not," said Margaret, more seriously; " I see what you mean. I will be careful what I say. But oh, she is truly disagreeable. Don't you think so yourself?"

"I don't think her very agreeable. But she may not think me so, and we have nothing to do with one another."

"But poor Mary has. I do so pity her. She was so glad to see me that she cried a little. I'm so glad I came! I told her what you said; and since you are so very kind, she would like very much indeed for me to come down to-morrow, to stay to the end of the week, to sleep here, and to be with her all day."

"I am very glad of it."

"Thank you. Then I will come down to-morrow. I am sure papa and mamma will let me, since John wants it too. I only saw him at luncheon. I was going to say something cheerful to him, when he glanced at Miss Brooke, and I looked at her too, and saw her sitting—this way.

Instead of saying grace like other people, and then eating whatever there was thankfully, she was in contemplation. I could hardly help staring, rude as it would have been."

"It is easy to see she is no great favourite of yours, or of Mary's; but since she is Mr. Brooke's sister, you know he may have the same affectionate feeling for her that Mary has for you; therefore if you come down here, I strongly advise you to overlook her tiresome ways, whatever they are. My belief is, that if they are taken no notice of, she will be all the more likely to get rid of them."

"Yes, that is true, no doubt," said Margaret. "I think they are chiefly done for effect."

"And now I will go with you to the railway station."

CHAPTER IV.

MINISTERING WOMEN.

"Order and cleanliness, and thought and care,
The hush of quiet, or the sound of prayer."
THE HON. MRS. NORTON—"*The Lady of La Garaye.*"

WHEN Miss Beaumorice awoke the next morning, it was with a vague consciousness that she had something painful to go through; and on remembering what it was, she breathed a heartfelt prayer that Mrs. Caryl might have strength for her day. How glad she afterwards was that she had done this!

After breakfast, she desired her guest-room to be prepared for Margaret, gave her orders for the day, left the time of her own return uncertain, and started on her mission of friendship with a little basket containing the beef-jelly, which, after being well skimmed, proved as firm, clear, and tasteless as calf's foot.

Arriving at Mrs. Caryl's, she found her on the sofa as before, but looking as if she had had a world of heart-searching in the interim, and had sought and found help where it is never asked in vain. The little they said to one another was serious but not sad ; to beguile the tedium of waiting for Mr. Finch, Miss Beaumorice offered to read ; and Mrs. Caryl directed her to a particular portion to which she listened with sedate composure. Silence ensued ; and then she was prevailed on to take some of the jelly, which she found very palatable and sustaining.

The reader need not be harassed with details of suffering endured long ago ; it need only be said that Miss Beaumorice had seldom taken part in a more trying scene; and that her courage and calmness being equal to the unexpected occasion, she proved an inestimable comfort to her afflicted friend. Mr. Finch, a man not addicted to frequent praise, could not refrain from a few words of hearty admiration of Mrs. Caryl's fortitude; and gave minute directions, with the utmost kindness, how her case was to be alleviated and watched. He suggested the expedience of engaging a professional nurse, to which Mrs. Caryl was evidently reluctant; and Miss Beaumorice set the question at rest by engaging to remain with her herself as long as wanted.

When he was gone Mrs. Caryl shed a few natural tears, which she even apologized for, saying she had been wound up rather too long—it was only a passing weakness.

"How can you call yourself weak ?" said Miss Beaumorice. "*I* cannot call you so."

"It *is* weak nevertheless, to be affected at an end for which I have so long been preparing. What is there I should live for now ?"

"Do you remember Christian and Hopeful, when they reached the border of the great river ? Christian could not see his way clearly before him, and in a great measure lost his memory and good sense ; for he could no longer recall the encouragements he had received throughout his pilgrimage."

"Go on, please."

"All the words he spoke discovered horror of mind and heart-fears, — that he should die in the river, and never obtain entrance through the strait gate on the other side. In vain Hopeful cried cheerfully, 'Brother, I see the gate, and men standing by to receive us!' Do you remember Christian's sorrowful answer? ''Tis you, 'tis you they are waiting for!' Then Hopeful said, ' All these troubles and distresses of yours are no sign that God has forsaken you; but are sent to try whether you remember or have forgotten the many helps in time of trouble, which you had received before.'"

"Ah! indeed I have," said Mrs. Caryl, emphatically, "and it is a shame I should have so little faith now. Thank you, dear friend."

Miss Beaumorice afterwards asked her whether there were any letters to write.

"Not to Edith to-day," said Mrs. Caryl. "You may think I stave it off; but it is for the chance of having something more hopeful to tell to-morrow, or perhaps no need to say anything at all. I am so reluctant to pain my brother! And if I do not write, he will only attribute it to some little hindrance. Those other letters," she added presently, " will amuse me when I get better—if I do get better."

Miss Beaumorice had brought some work, which gave the excuse of employment when needed, without any noise or fuss, and while thus quietly occupied, she had the satisfaction of seeing Mrs. Caryl fall into a peaceful sleep, which lasted a long time. When she woke she said, thankfully,—

" I feel ever so much better—quite another thing—quite hopeful. I am sure all is ordered for the best."

Early in the afternoon, Mrs. Garrow called. Her manner was so much softer and quieter than usual that it showed her an adept in nursing. She said, " I am so sorry for what you have suffered. I have just seen Mr. Finch and he has sent me here. You know my old nurse, Hancock ?"

"Oh yes, very well. A very nice creature."

" She has just come to me for a month,
on invitation, to make herself generally
useful. Now if you like to have her for a
short time, she will be no expense to you
except her board, and I think you will find
her very handy."

"Yes, I am sure I should," said Mrs.
Caryl, "and then I shall not be a tax on
dear Miss Beaumorice. Not a word, my
dear friend! This provision is really providential. Nurse Hancock has strength to
lift me, and is accustomed to illnesses; she
can sleep at any time of day, and wake any
time of night. You must still pay me kind
visits and watch me, read and write letters,
correct proofs and post them; so you see I
have fully enough for two pair of hands,"
and she drew her gently down to her and
kissed her.

" Yes, that will be the nicest plan possible," said Mrs. Garrow; "for nurse Hancock, whatever may be her other qualifications, can neither correct proofs nor write letters, nor read a chapter without a good many blunders. Otherwise, the nicest creature !—Mr. Finch wishes it, and begged me to arrange it."

"So be it then," said Miss Beaumorice, " if you indeed wish it, dear Mrs. Caryl."

"Yes, I do indeed," squeezing her hand.

" But you may rely on my daily visits to make myself as useful and acceptable as I can, while Mrs. Hancock undertakes the night watches."

"I shall be so grateful to you !—when your health and the weather permit. I feel a load taken off me."

Mrs. Garrow had the tact not to stay too long, and said nurse Hancock should come as soon as she got home. Miss Beaumorice engaged to await her arrival.

When she came, she proved to be such a sweet-looking old woman! She must have been exceedingly pretty in her youth, and had much of the better part of beauty left. She was *not*—

' "Sans teeth, sans eyes, sans ears, sans everything."

Her sight and hearing were quite good, her hair scarcely silvered, her figure compact and active, her voice remarkably pleasant. Miss Beaumorice took to her directly, and Mrs. Caryl welcomed her like an old friend.

Leaving them to their afternoon tea with everything comfortable about them, Miss Beaumorice bent her steps homeward, and felt rather overcome when she first found herself in the open air. A few tears relieved her; she was glad to get rid of them as a party of merry little children came in sight, with nursemaid, and a perambulator. They were the young Finches; lovely enough to paint.

Margaret was awaiting Miss Beaumorice. She said,—

"Oh, how sorry I am to hear how you have been engaged! Mr. Finch told us of it when he saw Mary, and he seemed quite affected when he spoke of Mrs. Caryl's fortitude and your kindness. Poor woman! we were very sorry for her. The worst is, that when Susan heard of her illness, it upset her completely; and she said she must leave Mary and go and wait on her. Of course that could not be allowed, and Mary was very much vexed with [her; so she has been crying all day."

"Susan will comfort herself when she hears that Mrs. Garrow has sent her excellent nurse, Hancock, to wait on Mrs. Caryl," said Miss Beaumorice, "therefore be sure you tell her of it in the morning."

"Yes, I will, though she very likely will hear of it meanwhile," said Margaret; "for

James was going to take a card with kind inquiries.   Susan wanted to go herself."

"It is pleasing to see she has such an affectionate heart."

"It would be more so, though, if her affection were for Mary."

"Think how much longer she has lived with Mrs. Caryl!   In time she may have the same feeling for Mary.   I hope she will."

"Yes; and she really is very good and obliging to Mary—this has been the only thing to complain of."

"And you think dear Mary better?"

"Decidedly; though Mr. Finch will not let her leave her bed yet.   I don't think she much wants to do so, because she is now more out of Alicia Brooke's way. What a good thing, Miss Beaumorice, that half her month is over!"

"Are you sure she will leave at the month's end?"

" Indeed I am afraid of making too sure of it; but she has not been asked, *yet*, to stay longer; and Mary is talking of little things she shall do when Alicia is gone— just as she did about me! *That* may not hinder John from asking her to stay longer, you know; so we must be prepared for the worst! At first, Mary says, he even wished she should come and live with them altogether; which would have been horrible. But Mary said very firmly, ' No, love, you must never expect me to have a boarder.' Mary can be very firm when she chooses; and John is very reasonable. Still, he was a good deal taken with Alicia at first, especially as she used to flatter him so abominably, and pass herself off for such a saint. But he is rather disenchanted now —chiefly, I think, by her saying she should like to attend a course of anatomy, and visit a dissecting room. That disgusted him very much; and at first she was not quick enough to see it. Mary thinks it was only talk ; and does not believe Alicia has nerve enough for anything of the kind.”

“ Some have a vocation,” said Miss Beaumorice, “ others mistake their vocation. I think there can be no doubt that Miss Nightingale had a real, decided vocation. She went on, firmly, fearlessly ; no more minding the voices that opposed and ridiculed her, than Princess Parizade when she had stuffed her ears with cotton.”

“ Ah ! one would like to be a Florence Nightingale !” said Margaret. “ But few can even approach her—certainly not Miss Brooke. And then she had such efficient helps ; and the crisis was so important and uncommon. Whenever anybody does something very grand, there are always so many inferior imitators.”

“ At all events, the class of nurses is thereby raised.”

" Yes. I should like to be a good nurse —a very good one. I used to dislike being even a few minutes in a sick room—so close and unpleasant ! It used to try me more than anybody knew, to be with any of the children when they were ill, though of course I did not show it. But now I should rather like overcoming feelings of that sort, and nursing others just as I should like to be nursed myself. There is no need to wear a particular dress for it."

" Not in your case, though in large institutions it is desirable to have rules for suitable clothing, that will wash, for instance, and not rustle, nor convey infection. It saves trouble to define these things, otherwise they would be frequently infringed ; but no good could be answered by adopting such head-dresses as those of he Béguines of Ghent, for example. With them it is the mark of a community—of avowed separation from the world ; which we endeavour to do without outward and visible sign."

"I used to think the nuns' dress so pretty! We acted a school play of Madame de Genlis', once—'Cécile'—and all the dresses were so pretty, except La Mère Opportune's, and hers was quaint, like a Béguine's."

"The dresses are, as you say, very pretty, and, in my opinion, a snare—fostering the very feelings they are intended to avoid. Perhaps one reason may be (though it sounds an absurd one), that men have had some share in devising them. I think it beyond the power of the cleverest man to know all the little ins and outs of the female heart, in spite of all the confessions in the world. Happy and safe for us, then, to carry our confessions to Him who knows all the ins and outs of our vain hearts already."

"It seems to me that vanity is the root

of all evil," said Margaret. "Quite as much so as money, though most people would laugh at me for saying so. I begin quite to love Mrs. Garrow. She paid such a kind visit to-day. I had her almost all to myself, for Miss Brooke does not seem *en rapport* with her. She offered to see Mary, but I dared not let her; and yet Mary said, afterwards, that she should have liked to see her; so next time, perhaps, she will. Mrs. Garrow was quite motherly. I like her calling me 'my dear,' though Mary does not. Perhaps that's because I'm not a married woman. Mrs. Garrow looked at some embroidery on the table, without asking whose it was, and said, 'For a vestment, I suppose? I don't approve of fallals. Don't waste your eyesight on them, my dear. The poor need it more than the clergy.' I was as near as could be saying, 'It is not mine,' but did not; and Alicia sat so prim, and never said a word!"

" Perhaps it was a good thing she did not—it might have led to something unpleasant."

" Perhaps Mrs. Garrow guessed who did it, all the time! I hope she did, for I do not want her to think it mine."

" Those little things generally clear themselves up, without our needing to put ourselves out of the way about them."

" She was so pleased that Mary liked her jelly so much, and said, ' My dear, the next time I make any, you shall come and see how it is made,' which is just what I shall like. Our cook at home does not like being interfered with, and besides, her jelly is not half so good. Surely it is very good for a clergyman's wife to be able to do all these things, Miss Beaumorice ? Not only to understand them, but to be able to use her own hands, if there is need."

" Indeed I think so, Margaret. During the last illness of the late Duke of Sutherland, his daughters prepared for him everything he took, themselves. If their dishes had been literally slops and messes, it would have been no kindness to him."

After a short pause Margaret began to laugh a little.

"It was so amusing," said she, abruptly; "Alicia did not know of my coming back to-day, because Mary had not mentioned it to her. In fact, it was not quite certain I could till I had seen papa and mamma. It was one of Alicia's soup days, and also her fast day, or what she chooses to call so. Mary says she does not eat a morsel at breakfast, nor ostensibly till dinner, except a dry crust at lunch. I arrived quite unexpectedly by her, and, the door being ajar, walked straight into the kitchen to look for Susan. There, by the kitchen fire, with her feet on the fender, sat Alicia very comfortably watching the digester, and at the same time enjoying—no other word is strong enough—enjoying a basin of her soup with a good thick slice of bread. I never was more surprised and diverted. She turned round, but could not speak till she had scalded her mouth, and coloured up so red! I could not help saying, 'Your soup smells very nice,' and left her. She had not a word to say. Mary did laugh so."

"You are too bad, Margaret," said Miss Beaumorice, unable to help laughing a little, too.

"I?" said Margaret. "*She* was, if you please. *I* had nothing to do but to see what I couldn't help seeing. I wish John had been there too. So that's the use of her charity soup! There won't be any more made for a while, though, for the Irishman has committed some misdemeanour, and been had up at the town hall, and he and his family are going to be deported to their own parish."

" A good thing for this parish, at any rate, if Miss Brooke does not pick up some fresh vagrants still less creditable."

" No ; John said at luncheon time, quite wearily, ' I would rather not have any more tramps brought to the house, Alicia, while Mary keeps her room. As long as she can look after her household herself the case is different ; but your goodness has been imposed on ; and while she is away and I am away, it is not pleasant to either of us.' "

" I am glad Mr. Brooke spoke so sensibly," said Miss Beaumorice.

" Oh, he always says just what is right when he knows how things really are ; it is that which made me wish he had seen the soup-luncheon this morning. Alicia was off to church directly afterwards. I should have gone to church too, had I been at home, but I had come down on purpose to be with Mary."

" What a fine evening it is !" said Miss

Beaumorice. "Would not you like to spend half an hour with the Miss Nunehams? or are you too tired?"

"*I* am not too tired, if you are not; but I hardly know them well enough to intrude on them by myself; and I am sure you must be too tired to want to go out again."

"No; the distance is not great, and I am pretty well rested. I should like it."

"I am sure I shall, then," said Margaret.

At Mr. Nuneham's they found a merry family party playing croquet on the lawn, while their grandmother sat at the open French window, placidly enjoying the scene. In addition to the young Nunehams, there was Mr. Frank Garrow, with whom Margaret had dined at the rectory. Mr. Nuneham, with a cup of tea in his hand, was alternately watching them and chatting with his mother. They all gave a very cordial reception to the new-comers; and Margaret was easily persuaded to join the young people, while Miss Beaumorice found her own place with Mrs. Nuneham and her son. Their talk soon became gravely interesting, beginning with Mrs. Caryl.

"We are very inconsistent in wanting to keep her still among us," said Mr. Nuneham, "when her better portion is awaiting her, and she has really so very little to tie her to this life. But that does not hinder us from wishing to enjoy her presence among us as long as we can; she is loved much by the few who know her, and there is a larger number who know her through her pen—a little circle, after all, but on whom her impress, as far as it goes, is not only blameless, but beneficial. Happy the author of whom as much can be said!— who, dying, leaves no line he fain would blot."

A violent assault was here made on Mr. Nuneham by some of his youngest children who were resolved he should take part in the game; and though his mother had not long before professed her inability to discover any sense or wit in it, yet directly he was drawn away to be a player, though but for five minutes, she became amused and interested in watching him.

"Do see what a boy he still is!" said she to Miss Beaumorice. "Not even the youngest children are fonder of a game of play than he is. It does him good, I know—changes the current of his thoughts—and there is Mr. Garrow to keep him in countenance—if he wants it."

Miss Beaumorice did not find it needful to call Margaret to go home till the full moon had risen; and then Mr. Garrow, and Arthur Nuneham, and Grace, and Julia accompanied them to Miss Beaumorice's little green gate.

CHAPTER V.

STRUGGLING THROUGH.

"I have been to a land, a border land,
　　Where there was but a strange dim light,
　Where shadows and dreams, in a spectral land,
　　Seemed real to the aching sight.
　I scarce bethought me how there I came,
　　Or if thence I should pass again,
　Its morning and night were marked by the flight
　　Or coming of woe and pain."—MRS. RANYARD.

I HAVE not said, nor did I mean to say, that they walked two and two like a boarding-school. Miss Beaumorice, Julia, and, at first, Arthur, took the lead, Margaret, Grace, and Mr. Garrow came afterwards; and when some compliments had been duly paid to the

moon, and some verses suitable or otherwise, quoted, Mr. Garrow said,—

"Miss Beaufort, my aunt has a message
for you, though she did not know I should
be happy enough to have the opportunity
of communicating it."

"What can it be?" said Margaret.

"She has secured some pigs' feet, or
sheeps' trotters, or calf's liver, or bullock's
heart, I really forget which——"

"Calves' feet, I am sure," said Margaret,
laughing.

"Yes, I really think it was; and if you
will come to her to-morrow, precisely at
ten o'clock, you will be initiated into some
magic mysteries."

"How lucky you should have remembered to tell me!"

"There was no luck in it, because I
could not remember what she had never
told me to do. But I happened most
cleverly to over-hear her saying, 'By-the-

bye, I must send word to that nice girl,'
—'or that charming girl, or that delightful girl, I cannot be sure of the exact
word.'"

"The first was most likely to be right."

"Well, no, I think it must have been
that delightful girl."

"That nice girl, most likely," said
Grace.

"Nothing so prosaic, I am certain,—nothing so flat, so unworthy."

"The long and short of it is," said Margaret, "that Mrs. Garrow is going to make
some jelly, and is kind enough to let me
see it made."

"Which she herself would be sure to let
you know of in time," said Grace, drily.

"Ten to one you will find a note or
message from her awaiting you when you
get home."

"Yes, I dare say I shall," said Margaret,
after a moment's consideration of some-

thing in Grace's tone that struck her not quite pleasantly.

"We are going to have an orchis hunt to-morrow evening," said Arthur, falling back to them. "How pleasant it would be if you could go with us! Would not it, Grace?"

"Yes," said Grace. "Will you come?"

"I should like it very much," said Margaret, "for I have never seen an orchis; but——"

"Never seen an orchis? Oh! then you really must come!" said Arthur.

"Yes, it is a case of necessity," said Mr. Garrow. "Every one ought to see an orchis who can."

"Unfortunately it is a case of necessity that my sister should have my attendance in her sick room, and I cannot forsake her for any orchis, however wonderful."

"What, not for a monkey-orchis? a regular orang-outang? or a lady-orchis in the costume of Queen Elizabeth ? or a gentleman-orchis, the image of Sir Walter Raleigh ?"

" I don't believe there are such orchises," said Margaret, laughing.

" No, there are not," said Grace, indignantly.

" Miss Grace ! what are you thinking of ? Do you mean to say there are no men-orchises, women-orchises, and monkey-orchises ?"

" None such as you are pretending. People ought to speak truth."

" Oh, now I'm shut up."

" But the bee-orchises are the most wonderful of all," interposed Arthur. " They really might be mistaken for bees, —and the fly-orchises, might they not, Mr. Garrow ?"

" Oh, I must not say a word," replied he, in a mock-melancholy voice, " I've been snubbed. My heart is broken."

"Nonsense," said Grace, softening, however.

"Miss Grace says I tell stories. I'm out of Miss Grace's good books."

"That will not break your heart, though. People should not exaggerate."

"How you floor poor fellows with your generalities! 'People shouldn't exaggerate. People ought to speak truth.' Of course people ought; but unless I am implied to be one of the people, the axiom has no point."

"Oh, well, don't let us think any more of it."

"But I can't help thinking more of it," replied he, laughing. "My character is implicated."

"How stupid!" muttered Grace, impatiently. "Shall we expect to see you to-morrow afternoon, Miss Beaufort?"

"I cannot say yes without consulting Miss Beaumorice," said Margaret. "I am her guest when I am not with my sister."

Here they reached Miss Beaumorice's gate. Miss Beaumorice and Julia were exchanging good-nights, when Margaret stepped forward, and said,—

"Miss Grace Nuneham has been kind enough to ask me to join some of her family in orchis-hunting to-morrow evening. May I go ?"

"Certainly, my dear, if you like it."

"It will be an afternoon rather than an evening engagement," said Grace, "for we shall drink tea very early. Perhaps you will come too, Miss Beaumorice."

"Thank you, I am not quite at liberty just now, and should probably be too tired."

"*You*, then, we will depend on," said Julia, heartily, to Margaret. "Come early : come a little before five."

"Thank you, I will."

They watched them to the turn of the road, and then went in.

"What a lovely summer evening!" cried Margaret. "Any letter or message for me, Jessy?"

"No, miss."

"Do you expect any?" said Miss Beaumorice, surprised.

"I just thought Mrs. Garrow might have sent one, because Mr. Garrow said she wanted me to go to her to-morrow morning at ten o'clock to see the jelly made."

"Oh! then you must go by all means."

"I must explain afterwards to Mary. I am so glad of this orchis party. I wanted to see more of the Nunehams—they are so nice! Don't you think so?"

"Yes, I like them very much."

"Mr. Garrow is there very often, I suppose."

"No, I think not. He is not here very

often, but he is on very good terms with them."

" Is he engaged to any one of them, do you think ?"

" Oh, dear no ! I have not an idea of it. The Nunehams are not flirting girls."

" No, I can see that ; but it need not hinder them all their lives from being engaged."

" Certainly not ; but I don't believe such a thought has entered their head,—in a serious way, that is. They are very simple-minded ; not at all addicted to receiving or expecting attention or admiration."

" That may make them more deserving of it, though," said Margaret.

" Certainly. And I should be very glad, indeed, to hear of any one of them being engaged to a deserving man some of these days. But he must drop from the skies, I think."

Margaret saw no reason he should fall

from such a height, but did not say so.
After a light supper they went to bed
early.

At breakfast next morning they were
settling their plans, and arranging to walk
together to Mrs. Caryl's gate, and for Margaret then to proceed to the rectory, when
they were surprised by a ring at the
visitor's bell, and the next minute Mr.
Garrow was announced. After exchanging
greetings with Miss Beaumorice, he turned
to Margaret, and said, merrily,—

"I come to do penance. A precious
bungle I have made! and a fine scolding I
have had for my pains! My aunt is *not*
going to make jelly to-day, but to-morrow,
and says I had no business to interfere in
the matter, as she would have sent you
word in good time; so, as a punishment
for my misdemeanour, she has sent me to
tell you so, lest it might disarrange any of
your engagements."

They all laughed; and he said,—

"This will teach me not to be so officious again; but really I fancied I was doing a clever thing."

"Which officious people generally *do* fancy, perhaps," said Miss Beaumorice.

"Perhaps so. However, I hope the blunder has not been of any consequence."

"None whatever."

"All's right, then—and even, if it had been, I am persuaded Miss Beaufort would have been good enough to forgive me."

"I don't know about that," said Margaret, "so pray don't make the experiment."

"No, no; 'A scalded dog fears cold water,' as the Italian proverb says. My aunt has been too sharp on me to tempt me to incur such a rap on the knuckles again. I am on my way to London now, by the 8.45; is there anything I can have the pleasure of doing for you?"

"Nothing, thank you," said Miss Beau-morice.

"Nor for you, Miss Beaufort ?"

"How could you expect me to trust you with anything ?" said Margaret, smiling.

"Well, I hope my character is not so irretrievably lost that I can never recover it.   If there *is* anything I can do for you I will try to do it well."

"There is nothing, thank you.   You are not going to be one of the orchis-hunting party, then ?"

"That would interfere with domestic arrangements.   Dr. and Mrs. Garrow will be just on the point of sitting down to dinner, and if I meet an old college friend I am expecting to see, I may dine and sleep in London.   I shall think of you all the same.   I shall think of you hunting with perseverance worthy of a better object, for an orchis like Queen Elizabeth or like Sir Walter Raleigh."

" I don't believe there are any men and women orchises," said Margaret.

"Oh, yes, there are," said Miss Beaumorice, "only they require a good deal of make-believe. Hear this,"—and she took down Withering's " Botany,"—"' Monkey orchis, — lip of the nectary five-lobed, downy; four of the lobes equal, linear, entire ; spur blunt, &c. Smells like woodruff when drying. Perennial; flowers in May; grows on chalk hills in England.'"

" There, now !" said Mr. Garrow, triumphantly.

" ' The lizard-orchis does not flower till July,'" pursued Miss Beaumorice, still referring to her book ; "' nor the frog-orchis and butterfly-orchis till June.' You will now only find the monkey, and green-winged meadow, and early purple, and great brown-winged, and military orchis. I can find no mention of the man and woman orchises in ' Withering.'"

"That confirms me in thinking them fabulous," said Margaret.

"But I have *seen* them," said Miss Beaumorice, smiling. "I own that a good deal of allowance must be made for them. Stay, I have found the man-orchis, under the head Aceras. It flowers in June. The man is something like a miniature representation of a man cut out of white paper."

"'Very like a whale,' and like Sir Walter Raleigh; as you will own when you see him, Miss Beaufort. Well, I wish you a pleasant orchis-hunt. How Miss Grace Nuneham fired up when she thought I was trying to impose on you!"

"She is very matter-of-fact," said Margaret, "but I think that I like her all the better for it."

"Oh, yes! but she was very amusing. Some people cannot take a joke. I believe her feeling was that a clergyman should not carry a joke too far; but I hope I was not doing so. I respect the principle, though, all the same."

It was time for him to start; and he was soon off. Margaret occupied herself for about an hour in dipping into the books on the bookshelves in her bedroom till Miss Beaumorice was ready for her.

"Now I am at your service," said Miss Beaumorice at length. "My little home duties are over for the present. You have not found the time hang heavy, I hope."

"No, I never do when I have a new store of books to look over," said Margaret; "and you have many that I should like to read. Milman's dramatic poems, for instance, and Mrs. Heman's life by her sister—those are what interested me this morning,—and Erskine Neale's ' Closing Scene,' and some others."

"You had better stay here till you have read them all," said Miss Beaumorice.

"Oh, that I might !" said Margaret.

"And then you could begin on Dr. Garrow's books, and after that on Mr. Nuneham's."

"Then they would call me a book-devourer, a literal book-worm, I suppose."

"They might call you something worse ; and I don't know who ' they ' means."

"Everybody, I think ; everybody who knows me at all, at least. At home I am sure they would."

"Well, I don't think you will trouble our clergymen's shelves yet, if you go through mine first."

"I dare say the Miss Nunehams have some nice books of their own, more in my way than Mr. Nuneham's. Do you think," said Margaret after a pause, "Miss Grace Nuneham is as good-tempered as her sisters ?"

"Yes, quite," said Miss Beaumorice, "I have never seen her temper ruffled in the least."

" I am glad of that."

" Have you ?"

" No ; perhaps not. She spoke rather sharply yesterday evening to Mr. Garrow, I thought, without occasion for it. But if she thought there *was* occasion, that made all the difference."

" Yes, all the difference," said Miss Beaumorice.

" He was running on rather amusingly, and I thought harmlessly, and she took it more seriously than she need."

" Ah ! they have been brought up differently. His views are naturally broader than hers. I do not say whether they are better or worse."

" But you *think*——"

" I dislike judging my friends dogmatically :—

" ' Let each give credit to his neighbour's share,
    But analyze his own with utmost care.'"

" Yes, that must be best," said Mar-

garet; " I think Miss Grace Nuneham——"

" You must analyze yourself, not her,
remember," said Miss Beaumorice, smiling.

When they reached Mrs. Caryl's door,
Margaret waited to hear how she had
passed the night. The report was a bad
one. She had been in great pain and very
feverish; Mr. Finch had seen her early.
She was still in bed, and was hoping to see
Miss Beaumorice.

She looked tolerably cheerful after all,
though worn and wan, and had letters and
newspapers before her.

" I am trying to amuse myself, you see,"
said she, holding out her hand with a smile.
" It does one no good to brood on one's
pains, *that* I have long been assured of. It
was what the Israelites did when they
were bitten by serpents. *That* did them
no good. 'They looked unto Him and

were lightened ' of their load of pain, fear, and grief."

"I do not wonder at their exceeding reverence for the brazen serpent ever after," said Miss Beaumorice; "and yet it became superstitious, almost idolatrous, at last. Hezekiah, therefore, acted like a strong-minded believer in breaking it up and calling it 'a mere thing of brass.' Perhaps many expected that condign punishment would fall upon him for it, but it did not. He took away the symbol because it interrupted their view of Him whom it symbolized. I am so thankful that you are trying to amuse yourself, dear friend."

"Read what I have just come to," said Mrs. Caryl, "in a number of the *Animal World*,* which a friend has just sent me."

She pointed out the passage, and then

* No. 22, Vol. ii., p. 156.

leant back on her pillows to rest, while Miss Beaumorice read to herself as follows :—

"Man's chief sufferings arise from his powerful self-consciousness; he cannot *forget* while in possession of those powers which raise him above the brute creation. His great nervous sensibility so vividly retains and so accurately transmits its impressions, that when his hand is off he may still fancy that he feels a pain in the lost fingers; it is but fancy, still the sensation is real. So with the living fingers,—pinch one, and he declares that he feels pain in the finger. This, however, is mere fancy also, for the real sensation is in the brain."

"I can't realize that," said Miss Beaumorice.

"It is true, though, no doubt," said Mrs. Caryl, smiling. "The question is, can the knowledge of it make one feel the pain one whit the less ?   I have a fair opportunity of trying.   At present I cannot say it has made my pain any better to tell myself, 'it is not *here*, but *here*.'   But one thing I *have* found, that the more I think of other things and other people, the less sensible I am of having any pain *at all*.

"There was a dear little boy I once knew," she added presently, "the son of Admiral Gardiner,—he fell from a pear-tree, and sustained a dreadful compound fracture.   There was no help for it but amputation at the hip-joint.   He bore it without so much as saying, 'oh.'"

"Brave little fellow !"

"He has been dead many years.   What are you smiling at ?"

"I came to amuse you if I could, and you are amusing *me*.   Interesting me would be the better expression."

"All in the day's work," said Mrs. Caryl.

"Sometimes it rests us as much to talk as at other times to be silent. I think a nurse never shows greater judgment than in knowing which is the case. Sometimes a check, when you are longing to say something, is the greatest worry! At another time the most amusing, the most interesting news conveys no pleasure.

"Is that nice young girl still with you?" she presently asked.

"Yes, she accompanied me to your door to hear how you were this morning, on her way to her sister."

"When I get better (if I ever get better) I should like you to bring her in some day, if she does not mind it. I should like to make nearer acquaintance with her frank young face."

"I am sure it will give her great pleasure to know you."

" I am not so sure of that ; but, at any rate, I will not claim much of her. Now, my dear friend, will you kindly make those corrections in ink which I have made scarcely legible in pencil?" and she gave her some proofs. As Miss Beaumorice took them and prepared to go down-stairs, she asked if she should summon Nurse Hancock.

" No, she is making up for her sleepless night by a sound sleep without the aid of ' Joan silverpin.' That is the old country name, you know, for the white poppy that the doctors use for narcotics. It reminded some one, I suppose, of the long hair-pins topped with silver balls that girls sometimes used. I feel as if I should sleep too." And she slept almost immediately.

Miss Beaumorice met Nurse Hancock stealing noiselessly in, and left her in charge to summon her when wanted.   A long stillness ensued.

Miss Beaumorice only remained a short time with Mrs. Caryl on her waking, fearing to tire her by much talking, and posted her proofs for her on her way home. She rather regretted that Miss Caryl was not yet written to, as she herself knew so little of Mrs. Caryl's antecedents : but she concluded Mr. Finch would advise it if necessary.

"How many pages there are in every one's inner life," thought she, "that others know nothing whatever about ! Doubtless it is best so, though some lives seem peculiarly lonely.   Only in a better world shall we 'know even as we are known,' nor can we even desire it to be otherwise."

When Margaret returned she brought the welcome intelligence that Mary was decidedly better, and promoted to a couch in her bedroom.

"So much pleasanter, you know, in this warm weather, and so much less invalidish. And another good thing I have to tell,— Miss Brooke is going away, for a few days at any rate. Her friend at St. Issy's has sent her a pressing invitation, which she was making a merit of refusing on Mary's account; but Mary so strenuously insisted on not being the obstacle, that she has been induced to decide on going for two days at any rate, since, as she truly says, Mary does not want two nurses, especially now she is getting better. So, to-morrow, when I go there, I expect to find Miss Brooke gone. And Mary begged me to say she hoped you would look in on her the day after, as it is quite an age since she has seen you. I can sleep there to-morrow, you know, in Miss Brooke's room, —in what is her room *now*, though it always seems to me she is sleeping in *mine.*"

" Has Mary made this arrangement ?"

" No, and it did not occur to me till I was returning."

" If Mary does not think it a good plan, then, you had better not press it, but return here as before."

" Thank you, dear Miss Beaumorice, I will gladly do so, but I think she certainly will. I suppose it is almost time for me to go to the Vicarage."

" No, they will hardly expect you yet. I think you may allow yourself an hour's rest and quiet with some nice book ; and you shall have an early cup of tea before you start on your orchis-hunt."

" Barkis is willing," said Margaret, laughing. And soon she was established in the bedroom bow-window, shaded with Venetian blinds, luxuriously ensconced in a great dimity-covered easy chair, with not one book, but three or four for her companions. Here we will leave her, perhaps to drop comfortably asleep, like Newton's " Girl at her Studies."

CHAPTER VI.

THE ORCHIS-HUNT.

" Real life is not dinner-parties or small-talk, nor even croquet and dancing."

EDWARD DENISON.

MARGARET would have afterwards told her special friends and sympathizers, if they had asked her, that orchis-hunting was one of the most delightful pursuits in the world; but it may be surmised that she would have said the same of truffle-hunting, crystal-hunting, or any other hunting, had the attending circumstances been the same. First, the young people were all in happy tune ; next, the evening was delightful ; then, the walk was charming ; and added to all was a halo of youth and a flow of good spirits that would have made enjoyment even if it had not found it.

"I came in for a second tea," she said afterwards to Miss Beaumorice, "and then we set off, Grace, Julia, and I, and Arthur and Harry, up a road I had never been before, which was dusty and shadeless at first. A turn of the road brought us to a turnpike, where a neat old woman was knitting, and a blackbird singing in a wicker cage. After that, the road gradually ascended with a steep chalk hill above us on one side, and below us on the other. Soon we came to an old farmhouse on such a steep descent that we were level with the chimneys. Here we struck off the road down a very steep path, affording us glimpses of scenery most pastoral and charming ; and two little cowboys were talking to each other in raised voices from opposite hills.   Then the orchis-hunt began, and we found so many, and such numbers of other flowers, that we did not leave off till moonlight.   You did not think me too late, did you ?"

" Oh no.   I had only just come in from the garden."

" We hardly knew how late it was, nor how far we had to walk back ; for we had strayed on and on.   Grace gave me quite a botanical lesson, and showed me the lobes, and the spur, and the nectary, and made me repeat after her again and again, so that I think it is quite hammered into me.   It was a good thing she did it when she did, for when Mr. Garrow came——"

" Mr. Garrow ?   Did he come, after all ?"

" Yes, by an evening train.   We were quite taken by surprise—at least I was. They did not seem so.   After that there was no more teaching, for they only talked nonsense; at any rate nothing but give and take—serious on one side, bantering on the other."

"Unequal ?"

"Yes, because Grace would take things seriously that were really meant in joke."

"Rather dangerous."

"It might have been so: but Mr. Garrow just steered clear of that. At one time I thought he would make Grace really angry; I was in pain for her, lest she should show want of temper; and wondered it did not occur to her that he was trying to see how much she would bear."

"Not quite fair of him, either."

"At last he stopped short, and said quite in an altered voice, 'Miss Grace Nuneham, you have made quite a convert of me. I really did not think there was so much to be said on your side; and I don't believe you would have said it, or said it so well, if I had not pushed the argument further than perhaps I ought to have done. Pray forgive me!' and he held out his hand. She changed countenance and did not look up, or she would have seen how expressively he was looking at her. She gave him her hand rather reluctantly, I thought, and turned away to gather some more wild flowers. Mr. Garrow said, 'You have not forgiven me, you know.' 'Yes, I have.' 'Well, you did not say so, at any rate.' I thought that was a question they might settle together, and stepped forward and joined Julia. Presently Julia said, 'How beautifully the moon is rising. I suppose we ought to go home.'"

Miss Beaumorice laughed, and remarked—

"You have made more out of it, Margaret, than I could have done."

"I hope you don't think I have made something out of nothing."

"Oh, dear, no; it remains to see what the something is."

"Perhaps I ought not to see things sometimes. People tell me now and then that I fancy them. But I am very apt to get interested in persons, and I think that makes me rather quick-sighted."

"Or rather apt to fancy."

"That's what other people say," answered Margaret, quickly. Catching up her wild flowers she said, "I must put these in water at once, or they will be dead before morning. But, Miss Beaumorice, just let me go over one of them to you, that you may see I am quite right. See this mon-key-orchis; here are the five lobes of the nectary, four of them equal, linear, entire; the spur blunt, the leaves of the calyx taper and pointing."

"Quite right, Margaret."

"I was lucky to get them, I think, as they are so rare. I will show them to Mary to-morrow."

"You will go to Mrs. Garrow's first, I suppose. She has sent to say she shall expect you."

"Oh, yes, I will go there first. Mary does not really want me now, and Miss Brooke will not start till twelve. If she likes to stay with her dear friend Eulalia over Sunday, Mary will not mind it, nor shall I, if I am allowed to fill her place."

Next morning Margaret started in cheerful spirits, evidently anticipating a pleasant day, and she begged Miss Beaumorice not to expect her in the evening, unless she returned about the usual time, and to be sure to remember Mary's wish to see her on the following morning. The day passed uneventfully to Miss Beaumorice. She spent a few hours with Mrs. Caryl, who was very calm, but weak and drowsy; not equal to talking or to being much talked to. Nurse Hancock at her plain work seemed all the company she just then required. This enabled Miss Beaumorice to return home earlier than she might otherwise have done, and bestow some hours desirably.on her own affairs. In the evening, as Margaret did not make her appearance, she had leisure for reading.

She did not neglect her promise to call next day on Mary. It was easy to see by Susan's face when she opened the door that things wore a more cheerful aspect. To Miss Beaumorice's surprise and pleasure Mary was in the drawing-room, though carefully guarded from draught.

"You did not expect to find me here," said she, smiling and kissing Miss Beaumorice. "Mr. Finch gave me leave yesterday, so I came down directly Alicia was gone. I am so glad, so thankful, to be down here again."

"I am sure you must be."

"Yes; and——"

Here Margaret came in, with a broad smile on her face that was ready to become a laugh.

"Are you not glad Mary is down?" cried she, delightedly. "Oh, everything is going on so famously!"

Mary looked amused.

"Margaret, do tell Miss Beaumorice," said she, smiling, "or she will not be *au courant.*"

"Why, you must know," said Margaret, merrily, "that after a very pleasant morning with Mrs. Garrow, who made me thoroughly understand how to make jelly, I came here just after Miss Brooke was gone. Mary immediately proposed coming downstairs; so I made everything comfortable for her, and then brought her down. We both enjoyed being to ourselves, I must say, without a third party. And so then, when Mary was rested a little and had taken some refreshment, I put the question, 'Might I not in Miss Brooke's absence remain here till to-morrow?' She said 'Yes, if I liked, there would be no trouble except getting out clean sheets and towelling;' so I went upstairs to take them out, when I had taken off my things in my own room. It was rather in a litter, as if Miss Brooke had been very busy packing, too busy to leave it very tidy; and I thought Susan would arrange all that when she put on the sheets. I went to the closet where I used to hang up my bonnet, forgetful that it might now contain things that did not belong to me. It had never been locked in my time, and I did not know it had been since. However, it seems Alicia always locked it, but in her hurry lest she should lose the train (for John was calling to her that she was late), she never noticed that the lock had overshot the catch; so instead of having locked the door before pocketing the key, it would not lock or even close."

"I see," said Miss Beaumorice, mystified.

"So, there," pursued Margaret in glee, "I opened the door without thinking of anything, and in a moment saw what I ought never to have seen! not only books, bags, baskets, but biscuits, jams, preserved meats—oh, such a *cache!*"

Mary here burst into an irrepressible fit of laughter, in which Miss Beaumorice, though scandalized, could not help joining.

"Margaret, you are too bad," said she, the next moment, trying to look reproachfully.

"I? *she* is, you mean," said Margaret; "why will you always put the cap on the wrong head? I haven't been hiding eatables and pretending I was fasting. *I* have only had the misfortune, if you will call it so, of finding out quite undoubtedly, that *she* did."

"No misfortune at all, I think," said Mary. "I call it quite a fortunate discovery. Here has been Alicia acting a part and pretending to be quite different from what she really was, and quite superior to everybody else, and everybody else so very much worse, and now she's found out. I do hate deceit."

"So do I," said Miss Beaumorice, " and—"

"You should have seen John's face when I told him," pursued Mary. "He thought much more of it than I expected. At first I was afraid he would be angry; and so he was, but not with us. But he would not say a word after the first exclamation. I wanted him to use his own eyes, but he would not. I would not have missed his first look for the world, but after that he schooled his looks as well as his tongue."

"I admire him for that," said Miss Beaumorice. " You see, she is his sister."

"Oh, but that really is *no* excuse," said Mary. "Is she to do all manner of wrong things because she's his sister?"

"No, certainly not, only—dear me! it *was* rather unfortunate!" and Miss Beaumorice could not help laughing a little again.

"Do give a good hearty laugh, Miss Beaumorice," said Margaret, merrily. "I know you are longing to do it."

"No, indeed, Margaret; because, you see, I cannot help thinking what annoyance Miss Brooke will feel when——"

"She finds she's found out," interposed Mary. "Don't you think she deserves it?"

"If all have their deserts, who shall 'scape whipping? Perhaps the best way would be to say nothing about it."

"Oh, but indeed I *shall* say something, if only about the fasting woman of Tutbury. I've no notion of letting her go on so—it would be immoral, I think. Such an example! No, indeed, she has said all sorts of things—cutting ones, too—about being under bondage to the things of this life, and I know not what all."

"You would not retaliate?"

"Retaliate—no, but—

"'If to her share some female errors fall,—'"

"You can't go on, Miss Beaumorice," said Margaret, laughing.

"Well, no; but it would be more generous to leave her to the lessons of her own conscience."

"I don't believe it pricks her a bit," said Mary. "She has ways of quieting it."

"Poor Miss Brooke! she has been unwise, to say the least, to seek reputation in such a way, for I suppose that is what it all amounts to. I have known old ladies and invalids glad to have a biscuit or some such refreshment at hand, in case of feeling faint in the night, and in order not to disturb others."

"That's quite a different thing," said Mary; "absolutely different. That implies no deceit. The assumption of a self-denial that does not belong to her, and quietly accepting praise for it, is what has been Alicia's fault."

"Well, I admit that you are right. And now, having done so, let me beg you, dear Mary, not to trouble yourself any more about her delinquencies, or short-comings, or whatever may be laid to her charge. To her own Master she stands or falls; to Him also do we."

"Oh, that is such a grave view."

"But am not I at a grave time of life? And are not you in the honourable, responsible position of a clergyman's wife?"

" And therefore bound not to overlook offences."

" But yet to deal tenderly with the offender."

" That is true, too ; and do you know, Miss Beaumorice, I have had some very serious thoughts during this illness."

" My dear Mary, I am very glad indeed to hear it."

" Very serious, even solemn thoughts," pursued Mary, " quite different from those I used to have. I feel, as you say, that a clergyman's wife *has* an honourable place to fill, and *is* highly responsible. Mrs. Garrow made me feel this first—feel it strongly, I mean—and I thought a good deal about it on my pillow—only I did not see my way at all clearly ; I wished to do well, but I felt quite at sea."

" You are in the right track, though, I hope and believe. If you wish to do well, wish heartily, you must seek guidance from the wise and kind—like Mrs. Garrow, for instance ; and you must pray."

" Yes, I know that ; I feel it," said Mary in a low voice.

" And then I believe you will be guided almost insensibly, involuntarily, into the right path ; and you will take continually increasing interest in your life-work, and be of continually increasing interest and delight to your husband."

" Oh, that *will* be nice, Mary," said Margaret.

" Yes, very," said Mary, less heartily than her sister. " I suppose it will all come in time—might have come by this time if Alicia had not hindered so. Another provoking way of hers—"

" Oh, a truce with her provoking ways," said Miss Beaumorice, laughing. " I did not bargain to hear any more of them. Let me hear of your pleasant ways, and Margaret's, please, this morning."

Mary laughed, and yet seemed half inclined to go on, but was withheld by Susan's bringing her a note.

"Here's a note from Alicia!" said she, hastily running over it. "Famous!"

"What is it, Mary?" cried Margaret.

"Her dear Eulalia has dislocated her ankle; and it would be such a privilege to stay and devote herself to her, if I had not a prior claim; or indeed, if it were even possible, supposing I waived that with my wonted goodness—her serge dress and list slippers being locked up in her bedroom closet. I shall write to her at once," cried Mary, starting up, "and say, my dear Alicia, make no scruple of remaining on my account, nor yet for the other reason. My sister is kindly supplying your place, and I am much less in want of nursing than your suffering friend—and as for your dress and slippers, I will forward them by the next train, as you inadvertently left your closet door open."

Margaret looked delighted.

"Take care what you say," said Miss Beaumorice, anxiously, "people are so easily hurt."

"Why, I am doing the very things she wants," insisted Mary, "releasing her from her obligation to me, and sending her the things she needs. Go up, Margaret, and pack them up directly."

"I hope I shan't burn my fingers," said Margaret laughing, as she ran off.

"Well, I wish you well through it all," said Miss Beaumorice, rather ruefully, as she rose to take leave.

"Oh, it is all arranged to my hand," said Mary, her pen flying over the paper. "See, I am using the lovely little inkstand you gave me—and this gold pen was from John; he assured me it would write like the pen of a Lady Mary Wortley Montague, who possibly wrote a bad hand after all. I want to write my very best, now, though, —dot my i's, and mind my stops. I shan't mind anything if *she* stops. Famous, Margaret! you have not been long—Susan will give you string; better put a seal on the knot. Put 'immediate' on the outside."

"I hope that won't be *too* broad."

"Nonsense—of course not. We want to oblige her. Everything will be spoilt if it arrives too late. Put this note in. Ring for James. He will run off with it to the station."

Mary had quite a pink colour in her cheeks when Miss Beaumorice took leave of her, but she was hardly glad to notice it. There seemed too much feverish irritability still about her; and as she pursued her way homeward, she was haunted by the words, "ye know not what spirit ye are of."

What enmity is often shown in very

little things ! Mary and Alicia were evidently unsuited to each other in every respect ; and it was very happy for them that they were not bound to be each other's companions for life; that the arrangement suggested by Mr. Brooke had not been too hastily decided upon.   Many a young wife's peace is shipwrecked by a third party, before she and her husband are thoroughly well known to each other. Wherefore, let engaged young people beware of giving too long invitations beforehand ; and let dear friends beware of staying too long.   It is sometimes dangerous to be over-persuaded to extend a visit.

Miss Beaumorice looked in on Mrs. Caryl, on her way home, and found her with a harassed look, trying to correct in pencil a formidable heap of proofs.

" I suppose it will be presumption to offer you my help," said she wishfully.

" No, indeed, it will be very kind," said

Mrs. Caryl. "My head spins with pencilling corrections already; and yet it is very important to me that these proofs should not be delayed, for I want the book to pass through the press before the autumn trade dinner."

"Shall I go over the corrections in ink?"

"Do so, please—and afterwards let me see them; and then post them. It will trouble you though, sadly."

"Not at all; I shall like it, and it will do me good."

"In the way of technicalities, perhaps it may," said Mrs. Caryl, wearily. "I am very fond of it, myself, when I am well, but not now. Perhaps you would sooner take them home? You are nearer to the post, and it does not go out till evening."

"I think I had better make a beginning here at any rate, that I may ascertain how far I am equal to the work."

And she set to it with zeal. At first she

required certain instructions and directions from Mrs. Caryl; but at length she found the pencil marks sufficient; and after working patiently at one proof, she gave it for examination before beginning another, and was gratified to find that she had executed her task faultlessly.

"Yes, I see I can trust you," said Mrs. Caryl passing her hand over her eyes, "and I cannot trust myself. I become so sleepy and stupid now, after dinner—I believe it is partly owing to the medicine. You may as well take them away with you, dear friend, for I am good for no more head work, and shall only make blunders. The verbal corrections are indicated already, and I can leave all the literal ones to you."

Gladly, therefore, Miss Beaumorice put all the proofs in her bag and carried them home; and after an early tea, they proved a delightful occupation to her. She was beginning to take great interest in the work itself, which seemed of a higher class than anything Mrs. Caryl had yet done; and the pencilled corrections gave her a close insight into her mind, and made her feel how much more analytical it was than her own.

"Why is this alteration made?" she asked herself, "why is this word better than the first? Oh, I see; the same word occurs again further down—it is altered to prevent tautology. Here is a Shaksperian line that I must verify—I hardly think it is verbatim—yes, it is! I might have been sure of it; but it is best to be on the safe side. How easily she writes, and yet it would not be easy to me to write like her. This comparison is quite fresh, and not forced—not caught for the purpose, and stuck down with a pin like an impaled insect. I suppose the printers are short of capital C's, and so have used X for the nonce, all down the page; how absurd it looks! Here is an amusing blunder enough. Instead of " they found the poor girl lying insensible on the floor of a cavern," the printer has made it " tavern." Mrs. Caryl might well make this emphatic pencil mark. Here is something else she overlooked, though; the " fawn of Praxitiles !"

Miss Beaumorice, though she was hardly aware of it at the time, was in reality taking an excellent lesson in composition; all the more useful that it was partly self-teaching, and partly under the leading of a practised guide. She had undertaken the task from sheer good nature and helpfulness, but soon was sensible of advantage and keen pleasure from it. Thus she by no means hurried it over; and when she had read the proofs for the last time, and packed them for the book post, she would not deny herself the pleasure of posting them herself. " Love knows no load."

She liked her work, and liked being useful to her friends ; and as she returned from her little walk by bright moonlight, though the summer sun had not long set, she thought with satisfaction on the humble events that had united in making hers a well spent day.

And after all she had time to make herself a cap !—or what ladies of a certain age now conspire to call one, though their grandmothers would have scouted them for it. Many women can suit their own age and looks better themselves than any milliner can for them, and have a natural pleasure in the performance besides ; and though Alice and Jessy could produce very smart little head dresses that they thought would suit their mistress exactly, her complaint generally was that they were " too young." A daisy with a frill of lace round it did not seem quite enough.

CHAPTER VII.

ENJOYING THEMSELVES.

"' O, evenings, worthy of the gods !' exclaimed
The Sabine bard. ' O, evenings,' I reply,
' More to be prized and coveted than yours.'"

COWPER.

THE next intelligence that awaited Miss Beaumorice when she visited Mary, was that Alicia had hastily returned, packed up her properties, and carried them off. She had said very little, except that she was much wanted by her friend, and seemed ashamed and disposed to be angry, but maintained a wise reticence.

"Of course I rallied her a little," said

Mary, " but I saw it would not do. She held her tongue, and I held my tongue ; we exchanged a cold enough kiss, and she left her love for dear John, who, she knew, would require no excuse for her returning at once to dear Eulalia. So I feel as if relieved of a nightmare ; for we were not *en rapport.*"

Miss Beaumorice thought they might have been a little more so if they had tried ; but after all it must have been by the sacrifice of fixed ways of thinking, perhaps to the detriment of one or the other. It is not so much the strongest principle, sometimes, as the most persistent will that is victorious, to the annoyance, perhaps unhappiness of one or more. It therefore seemed a stumbling block removed from Mary's path, that one who created little differences between the husband and wife, had ended her visit in this summary manner.

The effect on Mary's health, temper, and spirits soon were manifest.   She and Margaret now seemed as happy together as the day was long ; and though Mr. Brooke was vexed at first at his sister's abrupt departure, he soon ceased to mind it, and appeared to take more interest than he had yet done in his parish work.

As for Mary, she now rather enjoyed the remaining immunities of invalidism even with the drawback of a lingering cough. She reclined on the couch, read amusing books, did a little light work, wrote notes, and began to walk in the garden, and then along the sheltered side of the road.   Her throat and chest were still weak, however, and, instead of the other visitors to whom she had looked forward, she found it best to retain Margaret.

Imprudent indulgence in the open air too late one evening, brought on her violent cough again, and obliged her to submit, though reluctantly, to Mr. Finch's renewed superintendence.

"It really is hard," said she piteously, to Miss Beaumorice, "but mamma will have it so. She was here yesterday. They have let the house and are going down to Lowestoft; and they thought it would be so nice for me to go down with them, leaving Alicia to look after John. But that would put me in a fever; and Mr. Finch luckily calling while mamma was here, put his veto at once on my going to Lowestoft, and said it would be too keen for me; if I went anywhere, it should be to Devonshire, or to the south of France. I should so like to go to the south of France!"

"Since that cannot be," said Miss Beaumorice, "we must try to nurse you into health at home."

"Surely, clergymen change places with one another sometimes?" said Margaret, "to the benefit of both. Perhaps some

Devonshire curate may like to come here."

"I dare say," said Mary, ironically, "where everything is fresh and pretty, and people are just beginning to know us and like us. How should I like the trampling of half-a-dozen children on my new stair carpets, I wonder! I know what sort of places Devonshire curates have to live in— lodgings, nine times out of ten, or very poor, third-rate, small houses, meagrely furnished. That would not be a change for the better."

"Except for the air."

"Air is not everything."

Which was so undeniable that Margaret was at a loss for an answer.

"I wish I might stay here and nurse you," said she, presently.

"That would not be Devonshire nor the south of France."

"No, of course."

" It's no use wishing for what we can't have ; only it *is* trying."

And Mary squeezed her eyelids together to keep back her tears.

" It's best not to think about it," said she.

" Much ; but not always very easy," said Miss Beaumorice. " Oh, did a girl come here this morning with some very nice dinner mats ?"

" Yes, and I bought some of her because she came from you ; and I wanted some besides. Otherwise they were not very cheap."

" Neither cheap nor dear, I think," said Miss Beaumorice, " but I am very glad you did her a good turn, for she needed and deserved it. That girl is rather interesting, I think."

And she gave an outline of her story, which quite diverted Mary's thoughts from herself.

"One would like to help her," she said.

"You *have* helped her; and so has Mrs. Garrow, and so have the Nunehams."

"And Miss Beaumorice," said Margaret, smiling.

"So that, though we cannot give a long pull, nor a strong pull, we may help her through her difficulty by pulling all together."

"I should like to help her above all things, if it were in my power. Nothing is in my power now—I meant to be so helpful to John, and so useful to the poor—and now I'm quite laid aside."

"That is a lesson of patience and submission we all of us need sometimes."

"I wish you could teach me to submit!"

"Content yourself for a time with little things—even knitting a child's sock."

"Well, I *can* do that—and I suppose they are always wanted. And I think," added Mary, with effort, after a long pause.

" I might give a sovereign (or at least half a sovereign) to that poor girl, if you think it would really do her good. I have two of papa's sovereigns still left."

" I think it would do her great good."

" Well, then, half a sovereign—no, a sovereign," said Mary, quickly, " since I named that first. Bring me my little box, Margaret, that I may not go back."

" Give what you are disposed in your own mind," said Miss Beaumorice.

" I *am* disposed. It will be a sort of little thank-offering, though I'm not well yet."

" Only better—but you *are* better ?"

" Yes, than I was upstairs."

" This will be a nice thank-offering indeed," said Miss Beaumorice, as Mary held out a new sovereign. " I will send her to you to receive it."

" Oh, no, please !"

" Then I dare say Margaret will like to take it to her."

"Oh, yes, very much," said Margaret, gladly. "I wish I could give a sovereign too. But I can give her half-a-crown."

"Betsy will roll in riches," said Mary.

"Perhaps your sovereign may help her towards a sewing machine," said Miss Beaumorice. "I know she thinks that if she had one she could keep herself."

"Well, that does seem something to aim at," said Mary, with more animation than she had shewn yet.

The self-approval induced by this benevolent action stimulated her the rest of the day; but next afternoon, when Miss Beaumorice took her some beautiful cut flowers that had been given her by Mrs. Garrow, Mary was quite down again, and instead of lavishing praises on them as she sometimes did on flowers, said,—

"They only bring painful thoughts. They remind me of the fields, and gardens, and greenhouses, that everybody else is able to enjoy; while I in this charming weather am shut up here!"

"There are two sides to everything," said Miss Beaumorice. "I have just seen a poor woman who has been shut up seven years."

"Oh, of course, you may cap every suffering with something ten times worse. I have the bad taste—bad feeling, I suppose, to be most alive to my own."

"When I reached Mrs. Caryl's this morning," said Miss Beaumorice, without replying directly to her, "I found a very nice wheel-chair at her gate, which kind Mrs. Garrow had lent her, and she was so pleased! She would not otherwise have thought it possible to get into the air, but we managed it very nicely; and where do you think she wished to go?"

"Oh, I don't know. To the post-office, very likely."

"To the church, though it was not

prayer day. She liked sitting in its shelter, and reading the psalms there; and there I left her, with the man resting under the hedge."

" Curious," said Mary.

" Nice," said Margaret.

" I think, Mary, if you would like it, Mrs. Garrow will send the chair to you next."

" Oh, not at all !" cried Mary. " I should not like it by any means."

" The head keeps the draught off nicely."

" Oh, I'm not thinking of the draught— I couldn't bear it. Margaret, where are you going ?"

" To pack up," said Margaret, regretfully. " I thought I had better do so while you had Miss Beaumorice with you."

" I can't bear to lose you—I can't think what I shall do without you. I'm sure I ought not to be left. It is not very kind of mamma to take you away."

"I don't think mamma knew you wished me to stay," said Margaret, stopping short at the door. "I'm sure I would gladly."

"Oh, it's all arranged now; and I don't want to prevent your going to the sea-side."

"I don't care a straw for the seaside," said Margaret. "Not a pin."

"Oh, I'm sure you do; and I'm sure they like having you. Papa would be quite dull without you."

"Not if he thought I was a comfort to you."

"Oh, yes, he would. You must go now, only I know I shall miss you."

"It is very pleasant to hear you say so —I mean, I can't help liking to find I am any use or comfort," said Margaret, "and I'm sure I'll come back directly you ask me."

"Yes, yes, I know you will; only I must not ask you."

Miss Beaumorice remained till Margaret's packing was finished and she was ready to start. The parting was very affectionate ; there were tears in the eyes of both sisters.

"You have come in just at the right time," said Miss Beaumorice, gladly, to Mr. Brooke, as he entered ; "to be a companion to Mary, now Margaret is going."

"Oh, I knew Mary would want me just now," said he, "and planned accordingly. I'll take care of her while you take care of Margaret."

Mary looked pleased, and they had the satisfaction of leaving her with a smile on her face.

"I'm so glad John came in," said Margaret to Miss Beaumorice, while Jem trudged on in advance with her carpet-bag. "Do you think we really need be very uneasy about Mary ?"

"Not very uneasy ; but yet rather uneasy," said Miss Beaumorice. "That is what I am myself. If she will but be tolerably prudent, I don't think we need fear hectic symptoms."

"Hectic symptoms! oh how terrible that sounds," cried Margaret. "If there should be the least appearance of them, I shall never know comfort."

"But, my dear girl, I said I hoped we need *not* fear them, and I am sorry I even named the word. Common prudence is all that Mary wants; and surely she may exercise that."

"I don't know, I'm sure," said Margaret, uneasily. "She is dreadfully imprudent sometimes; and then as easily frightened. Dear Miss Beaumorice, here is a horse running away! Let us stand close to the hedge."

It was rather a perilous occurrence. The horse had probably been stung by a fly and was lashed into fury by the flapping of the bridle and stirrups against his sides.   A lad in the distance, running very fast, seemed as he approached, to make him more restive.   More than once he wheeled round, and his heels were very near Miss Beaumorice and Margaret.   In the excitement of the moment, they could think of nothing less pressing ; but when the horse was caught and they were out of danger, Miss Beaumorice observed, " I fear we have lost the train."

" Oh, dear !" said Margaret : and they both began to post along the shadeless road to the station, as if their lives depended on winning the race.   No strength was wasted in talking till Miss Beaumorice said,—

" Here it comes !" and a puff of white smoke and shrill shriek of the steam whistle proclaimed the near approach of the train to the station.

" Can we save it ?"

" No, I think not."

" I will run.   Good-bye."

" And away flew Margaret : but the station was still a good way off; and there was scarcely a chance of her reaching it in time.   Miss Beaumorice continued walking on, sure that Margaret had lost the race ; and soon a shrill signal, succeeded by the usual puff-puff, showed she was right. Jem was soon seen emerging from the station, and Margaret and he had a short colloquy, after which he returned to the station to deposit the carpet bag, and she disconsolately walked towards her friend.

" Lost !" cried she ; " and the next train will not arrive till 6.40.   What shall I do ?"

" Return with me to tea," said Miss Beaumorice.   " There is no time for you to go back to Mary."

12—2

"No, I'm afraid not. Hark! there is another train coming!"

"Only a down train. There really will not be an up-train till 6.40."

"What can't be cured must be endured," said Margaret, dolefully.

"And therefore we may as well enjoy ourselves."

"What an excellent suggestion!" cried Margaret, laughing. "To be sure we will! I should certainly lose the next train if I returned to Mary, who fancies me comfortably on my way to Charing Cross; and there would be good-bye to say again; so we *will* enjoy ourselves!"

And Margaret's face shone so with the heroic resolution that when Jessy opened the door, she could not help smiling too, from sympathy.

"Let us have tea at once, Jessy," said Miss Beaumorice, with spirit. "Some strawberries and cream, please. Plenty of toast. And the marbled veal."

"What a nice tea we are going to have," said Margaret, throwing off her hat and then taking possession of the easy chair which she knew was *not* Miss Beaumorice's. "I went over to Betsy Jones with the sovereign yesterday, and you cannot imagine how grateful she was."

"I think I can."

"It was very good of Mary to give a whole sovereign, I thought, when she might have given half; for she is not very rich."

"I thought so too, and was ready to say half would do; but refrained from tarnishing her work. We should not check a horse in leaping a gate. And the effort was a leap, from self-gratification to self-denial. I do not think she will have reason to regret it."

"Especially if Betsy does get the sewing-machine; which she really thinks she shall. What is the price?"

"Oh, five or six pounds. I incline to think she will raise it. I am glad Mary has been the first."

"Not quite the first."

"The other sums were not large enough to make it seem feasible."

"I will make a sewing-machine of myself, since we are so snugly *téte-à-téte*, and mend my glove while you are making the tea—'infusing' it, the Scotch say."

"Who in the world is that?" said Miss Beaumorice, as the house-bell was smartly pulled.

"Somebody to interrupt us," said Margaret.

As the door opened, Miss Beaumorice exclaimed "Alured! is it you?"

"Unless we're both mistaken," said he, laughing as he shook hands with her heartily. When his eyes met Margaret's, he involuntarily said, " Oh !" and then bowed very courteously.

" You know each other ?" said Miss Beaumorice.

" If the lady knows me," said Alured. " It is not my privilege to say so first."

" We travelled on the railway together," said Margaret, with a little shyness that was pleasing.

" We most certainly did so, since you remember it."

" Miss Beaufort mentioned to me," said Miss Beaumorice, " that she had travelled with some one who knew me."

" If I had known at the time that Miss Beaufort knew you, I should have found it difficult to let her treat me as a perfect stranger."

" I felt rather guilty in doing so," said Margaret. " You might have said something you did not wish a friend of Miss Beaumorice's to hear."

" Why did not you, then, put it out of my power ?" said he, quickly.

" I did not much like.—It seemed not very likely."

" Not at all likely I should say anything derogatory to Miss Beaumorice," said Alured, laughing.

" Oh, no, I am sure of it, now."

" Well, Alured, you will have tea with us, of course.   We are obliged to be early, because Miss Beaufort travels by the next train."

" So do I," said he, " so I will take good care of her if she will let me.   I am on leave, and want to see grandmamma before I return to quarters to-morrow."

" How are you getting on now ?"

" At the depôt ?   Oh, well enough.   We are not worked very hard.   Each man's turn for guard comes about once a week or ten days, which is not very much.   I my-self have more hard work, because I'm not yet dismissed from drill, though I hope to be in a week or two. I have three hours' drill a day. Then I work at the drill-book by myself, three hours more; so there's a good slice of the day accounted for at once."

" Very fairly accounted for, too, I think !" said Miss Beaumorice. " I had no idea the drill-book gave you so much to do."

" I hope to be thorough master of drill before I have been very long in the service, for there really must be great pleasure in handling a large body of men when one can do it well."

" You speak of them as if they were machines," said Margaret.

" Well, they are so in a great measure. As far as my limited experience goes, the British soldier is a fine fellow when not drunk—but that is too often. Many of the non-commissioned officers, though, are highly intellectual."

"Alured, I am delighted," said Miss Beaumorice, "to find you taking such interest in your profession."

"Oh, not too much of that—in the main it is so dreadfully uninteresting. We all get very sick of it sometimes. Awful grumbling."

"And yet, if the enemy——"

"Aye, he'd give us something to do! The Musketry Instructor is hardly a 're-source of amusement refined and delightful,' like a young lady's album."

"I should think not!" said Margaret.

"Let me give you a few strawberries, Miss Beaufort."

"Help yourself, Alured," said Miss Beaumorice.

"Native produce, I suppose," said Alured. "Such a fine sort, and so deliciously fresh."

"Well, but, Alured, tell us some more of your goings on. Have you any nice friends?"

" Among the subs ? Oh no, except Ainslie. They're such a set of empty pates : never open a book unless they are obliged."

" You cannot have nice conversation, then, I'm afraid."

" Seldom ; it is chiefly of horses, dogs, and the small gossip of the neighbourhood. Most of them are hobbledehoys imbued with a strong admiration of what they think manly, and chiefly ambitious of being considered ' knowing cards '—good at billiards and cricket, plucky in the hunting-field, but not given to any more serious reading than ' Jack Hinton.' "

" But what a pity," said Miss Beaumorice, " that some of the elder officers do not take interest enough in the subalterns to lead the conversation a little, and allure to brighter and higher things."

" Well, you see, the elder ones are chiefly married, and only mess with us occasionally.

I think there's only one man at our mess over thirty. None of us are very aged; and there are two or three who talk perpetually such rubbish and gossip! I had a conversation with our military doctor the other day about the poor style of talk at mess, and he fully agreed with me about it, but could not see how to mend it; but for the next day or two, there was a great improvement at our end of the table, as a nicer set happened to get together. I'm sure I must bore you with all this," said he, suddenly, to Margaret, who had been listening intently.

Margaret started and said,—

" It interests me very much. Please go on."

Alured looked gratified, and said,—

" I don't talk much myself anywhere, you know; rather preferring listening when there's anything worth listening to. Ainslie and I have long talks sometimes."

"On Sundays, perhaps. How do you pass your Sundays?" inquired Miss Beaumorice.

"I don't know what most of the fellows do—knock about and flirt with barmaids at different hotels, I fancy. I don't see what they do because I always go to church a second time, or else take a long walk. Our first service, you know, is necessarily early, because it must be ended before the regular church service at eleven begins. *We* go at half-past eight with the soldiers. Then comes a long forenoon, which I enjoy immensely, as it is the only quiet time I have all the week for reading. Then I have luncheon and start for afternoon service, sometimes with a companion, sometimes alone. Many men go a second time to church besides myself; most of them take a long walk, and a good many are always to be found in the mess-room. In the evening Ainslie and I generally contrive to join each other and talk on an immensity of subjects."

"Alured, I cannot help thinking he must be a very nice friend for you."

"I am certain he is, I am only too thankful for such a one. Many of the subs would not drift in the aimless way they do if they had a friend like him. It does people good to talk over their crude ideas and opinions, and find how much or how little there is in them. We have tough debates sometimes."

"As for instance?"

"Well,—lotteries and sweepstakes, for instance. Neither of us can waste money on them, for we both have preciously little; but I don't know that exception can be taken to sweepstakes on any ground except that of wasting money which might be better used. *You* are both against me, I see; but to me it is an open question. I know that betting produces evil; but if a man is strong enough to resist the temptation to spend more than he can afford, I don't see why he should not venture within that limit if he chooses to risk it."

Miss Beaumorice uttered a regretful " Oh !"

" You're against me, I know. Miss Beaufort's looks speak. However, you will be glad to know that I only defend this theoretically. I have never betted in my life, except once a pair of gloves."

" I'm *very* glad of that," said Margaret, softly, almost with a sigh.

" I am very glad," said Miss Beaumorice.

" Ainslie is just like you," said Alured ; " he dislikes the element of chance ; and in the main, so do I ; as I ought to, after having seen the foreign gaming-tables. Still we argue the thing, partly for practice, and he generally has the best of it, though I incline to leaving people to their own consciences. Dancing and balls, again.

Many excellent people think them wrong. I don't do so at present; should I change my mind I shall give them up."

On this and other subjects there was so much to say that Alured and Margaret were certainly sorry when they left the tea-table.

CHAPTER VIII.

THE ENJOYMENT ENDED.

"Though the pleasures of London exceed
In number the days of the year,
Catharina, did nothing impede,
Would find herself happier here."—Cowper.

"IS not there time to take one turn round your pretty gar-den, Miss Beaumorice," said Alured, "before we start? It looks so different in its summer beauty to what it was at Christmas."

"Yes," she replied, "there is time."

In passing a side-table, Alured looked at the title of a book lying on it.

"'Milton,'" said he. "That puts me in

mind of Miss Partridge. You remember her catechizing me in 'Comus.' That was one of our examination-books, Miss Beaufort. Some of the others were—Hume's 'Reign of Queen Elizabeth,' Shakspere's 'Julius Cæsar,' Bacon's 'Essays,' and the 'Life of Lord Clarendon.'"

"A very easy, pleasant set of books, surely?" said Margaret.

"Ah, but we had to go through them analytically—to take them to pieces as you are doing to that flower. This arbour looks as if it were 'for talking age and whispering lovers made.' Let us sit down."

"Only for five minutes, then," said Miss Beaumorice.

"Only for five minutes. In some company the five minutes might pass very quickly."

"Well, we must time ourselves."

"You've seen Ainslie, Miss Beaumorice? Not much of him, though."

" No, because you diverted me so from him."

" That's too bad. Well, how do you think he has diverted himself ?—Miss Beaufort is busy dissecting that honeysuckle, so she won't hear—he has engaged himself to be married."

" No ? Surely that is rather imprudent ?"

" Specially so, considering he has only an ensigncy, and she not even that. However, except in a monetary point of view, I doubt if he could have done better, for she is a most charming girl—the eldest daughter of a country clergyman."

" You know her, then ?"

" Yes, since he gave me his confidence. It seems they have been engaged some time."

" So that is the subject of your long talks ?"

" Some of them. We could not have

one more interesting. There's no good doing a thing by halves ; so when he'd let the cat out of the bag, he was not easy till he had taken me over to Copsewood, and made me free of the house."

"It is not far, then, from your quarters ?"

"Oh, a goodish step, as country folks say. Not too far for men with an object."

"And yours was a glimpse of a nice family."

"A charming family. I know you would think so. Really if Ainslie had not taken up the ground there, I should have been inclined to try my luck myself."

"Alured !"

"I'm upon honour, now, you know. No danger. Besides, I rather think Ainslie is more fitted for her than I am, and that she is fitter for him than for me. But in the light of a sister, you know, she is very charming. The mother is dead ; there are a lot of children, and she is like a mother to them all. The prettiest thing you ever saw in your life."

"What is her name?"

"Ellen—Ellen Fleetwood. She is about eighteen. She is a great deal cleverer and better read than I am, but not than Ainslie; and it is so pretty to see how she looks up to him, and to her father. She is so humble-minded, and unaffected. The children delight in her. There never seems a cross word spoken in the house."

"Margaret, we must not lose the train again," said Miss Beaumorice. "The five minutes are up."

They all rose, and walked towards the station.

"You will have a nice cool evening for your journey. Much cooler than it was at your party."

"Much," said Margaret. "I am very glad I lost the train."

"Well, Alured, cannot you tell me some more of this nice girl?"

"Oh, yes, if you like to hear me. It is all very well, Miss Beaumorice, to talk about the imprudence of young subs. getting engaged, but if they are worth anything at all, it helps to keep them straight. See here, now; at some fashionable place, suppose, where there are public walks and seats overlooking the sea and so forth, and a parcel of silly girls always ready to make others as idle as themselves—it is dreadfully bad for the subs. If a quiet, lady-like, and clever girl, with principle at the bottom of her conduct, like Miss Fleetwood, for instance—be the nicest companion a man can have, which is certainly the case, I think the opposite is a perfect horror. To hear their thin voices and empty clatter gives me the doldrums."

Margaret could not help laughing.

"Oh, it's true," said Alured, seriously.

" It really does. The influence you ladies have on men, especially on officers, is perfectly astonishing."

" They ought to be very careful, then, what their influence is," said Miss Beaumorice.

" Just what I say. And the influence of such young ladies as—Ellen Fleetwood, for example, is immense. The Fleetwoods belong to a croquet club at Green Vale. A lot of young people play there sometimes, but I don't think Miss Fleetwood cares for it much, and I like her all the better, for more nonsense than enough goes on sometimes. Ainslie says the pleasantest times there are the winter evenings, about Blindman's Holiday, when it is too dark to do anything but talk—not dark enough for candles. I can quite believe it."

" What is she like ?" said Margaret, suddenly. " Miss Fleetwood, I mean."

" Rather tall and slender, with very

pretty brown eyes—my favourite colour; isn't it yours, Miss Beaumorice?"

"Perhaps it is," said Miss Beaumorice, smiling a little. "I am fond of blue eyes, too, and dark grey. In fact, any eyes that have a good expression."

"Oh, yes, because then they reveal the soul. Still, I like brown eyes, almost black, the best." And he looked earnestly at Margaret, whose eyes happened to be cast down.

"How soon we have come to the railway station!" said Alured. "I think the road is like the Irishman's rope that he was tired of pulling in—the end must have been cut off. Perhaps we shall get a good talk yet, on the platform."

But no, the time was just up, the train was just due, and the passengers were on the look-out for it. The usual bustle, hurry and flurry, the usual last words, warnings, hopes and cautions, the parting hand-shakings, and smiles, and they were off. Miss Beaumorice caught the last bright look of the two promising young persons, so full of hope and capability of enjoyment, and goodness, and usefulness, and happiness; and wished them well in their several courses through life, with all her heart.

"I am glad Margaret lost the former train," said she to herself, as she went home. "What a near thing it was!"

She had been glad to see her acquaintance, Mrs. Hyde, in the same carriage with them; as though Mrs. Hyde was perfectly commonplace, she was an unexceptionable chaperon, in case one should be supposed essential; but indeed Miss Beaumorice was so thoroughly sure of Alured in every way imaginable, that she had as little hesitation in trusting him to look after Margaret as she would have had in his looking after herself, had she been his companion.

Her thoughts of both were very pleasant. Their characters were so gradually ripening, without, as yet, losing any freshness; the pleasure they inspired her with was unalloyed.

She found awaiting her at home a book from the book club to which she belonged, that she much wished to read — Sir Samuel Baker's "Expedition to the Albert Nyanza;" so here was an interesting evening employment provided for her; and soon she was thoroughly engrossed in the adventures of the indomitable traveller, as he sallied from Kartoum with his incomparable wife, his faithful servant Johann, who was so soon to fall a victim to sickness, his black man Richarn, who began so ill and ended so well, his model boy Saat, and his long pile of worthless attendants who mutinied directly he was defenceless. The heroism of Lady Baker, who again and again succoured her husband and cowed his men assailants, alternately moved her to admiration, mirth, and pity; she read far on, till her head was full of African adventure, but not till she made acquaintance with the false Kamrasi, of whose impudent imposture Baker might have been warned, had he believed the faithful woman Bacheeta.

Next morning, letter-writing, house affairs, arranging fresh flowers in her vases, and newspaper reading, took an hour or so of her time after breakfast. She was beginning to think of going out, when a ring at the bell forewarned her of a visitor, and Mr. Brooke entered — his usually healthy brown and red exchanged for mortal paleness.

"Mary?" exclaimed she, seeing directly something was amiss.

"Yes—will you go to her? I shall be so thankful. I am off to town, directly; you have heard of the accident?"

"No !—what, on the railway ?" gasped she, as she remembered her last look of the two bright young faces.

"Yes—in the tunnel. I know nothing to a certainty of details, and the men at the station, you know, are always like mutes. I have not a minute to spare—go to Mary, please ; but don't breathe a word to her of it."

Miss Beaumorice turned very faint ; but she just managed to say, "I will be careful," and he, too pre-occupied to notice her paleness, hurried off. She sat down, and for a few minutes could not think, only feel. Then she rang the bell without rising ; and on Jessy's entering said with a deep sigh,

"Bring me everything I want in order to go out. Have you heard of the railway accident ?"

"No, ma'am," with great concern. "At least," with sudden recollection, "I remember hearing one boy call to another—'have you heard of the awful smash?' but I took no notice—I thought it was only some boys' nonsense."

" Mr. Brooke has gone off to learn what has happened"—with another deep sigh, which seemed her only relief. " He has asked me to go to Mrs. Brooke and remain with her till he returns, without alarming her."

" That will be very difficult," said Jessy, softly, as she hastened off to execute Miss Beaumorice's order. She soon returned; and Miss Beaumorice set out, but not at her usual pace.

" Those poor children !" thought she; and her eyes filled with tears. " I was taking it for granted that they are among the hurt; and yet they may not have had a scratch ! Please God it may be so."

Mr. Finch drove along, and checked his horse when he saw her.

"Have you heard of the railway acdent?" they both said at the same time.

"Yes," answered he, "I am off to Cowfield to see what is going on. Shocking, is not it? Much magnified, most likely."

"Mrs. Brooke's sister——"

"Was *she* in it? Sad, sad—not hurt, perhaps; keep Mrs. Brooke from being frightened, if you can."

She went on with a heavy heart.

When she reached the cottage, it required a little resolution to go in. Mary was arranging some flowers.

"Miss Beaumorice! This is an unexpected pleasure; somehow I did not think you would come to-day."

"Why not?" said Miss Beaumorice.

"Oh, I don't know—because you have been so often lately."

"You are not tired of me, I hope."

"No indeed! I can never be that. And

now Margaret is gone, you are doubly welcome. Why, how pale you look!"

"The heat perhaps. At my age, people are not expected to have much colour. It is not quite so warm, though, this morning. There is a nice air. Well, what are you about now? Any fancy work in hand? How is James going on? he does not give you much trouble, I hope?"

"Oh, by-the-by, Miss Beaumorice, I want to ask you something."

And Miss Beaumorice was heartily glad at Mary's choosing a subject for herself which preoccupied her too much to need any more on her companion's part than short mechanical answers. Suddenly Miss Beaumorice started, and Mary in surprise said, "What's the matter?"

"Mr. Brooke's voice—"

"Oh no, he is gone to the school (which Miss Beaumorice knew he had not;) we are quite safe from him till lunch."

"Safe, Mary! what an expression!"

"Ah, it's what we come to in time, you see," said Mary laughing. "Married women all have little things to do, they can best do by themselves."

"Don't fancy it only the case of married women. Your spinster experiences don't date so very long ago."

"No, indeed. Don't fancy me tired of John when he really is at leisure to be companionable—and when I am at leisure to attend to him. But if I want to complain to the laundress, or cast up my accounts and consider how to lessen them, I'm not quite at leisure for the most improving conversation in the world. So Margaret lost her train after all!"

"Yes," said Miss Beaumorice with a sudden heart-pang. "It was a pity— though she did not seem to mind it much. James told you, of course. Oh yes, she came back to tea with me; and Alured

Ward happened to drop in, and was going up by the next train, and so they went up together."

" Very nice," said Mary.

" Very," said Miss Beaumorice, faintly.

" I suppose they are all on their way to Lowestoft by this time."

" I suppose so,—I hope so."

" Well, I hope so too, since they were to go, but I shall miss Margaret dreadfully ; and she said she should drag at every mile a lengthening chain."

" Dear girl !"

" Don't you think she improves very much ? grows more womanly ?"

" Yes," said Miss Beaumorice, strongly ; " I was thinking of it as I came here. Her character is developing, and a very sweet one it is. This is partly owing to you, Mary, and Mr. Brooke ; partly owing to her having to fill your place at home ; your illness, too, brought her forward, made her think and feel."

Mary looked pleased, and said, " Yes, I think you are right."

Miss Beaumorice softly sighed.

" What are you sighing for ?"

" Did I sigh, my dear ? It was from habit, I suppose : I did not know I did so."

" Your habit is smiling rather than sighing," said Mary ; " I have remarked it sometimes, and thought it was because you have passed through the suspenses and mistakes and heart-troubles of youth, and landed in happy, well-spent middle-life."

" I am past middle-life. Only think what an age mine would be if it were doubled ! I should be almost a centenarian."

" Not quite that,—not that by many years. That's not John," said Mary quickly, as the gate slammed. " Have you anything to say to him ?"

" Oh, no !"

" I think you have, though. ' Father Francis, I've come to confess,' hey ? Seriously, you are a little nervous, and I shall give you a glass of wine."

But Miss Beaumorice flouted the idea, and said that if she poured one out she would have to drink it herself.

" Oh, I shall not have one before lunch, if I do then. I fancy I only take it from habit, and might as well leave it off."

" Not against Mr. Finch's orders ?"

" But Mr. Finch has not ordered ; not positively ; and I don't want to empty John's little cellar,—his ' little bin,' as he says Herrick would call it. Don't you notice that my cough is quieter this morning ?"

" Yes, it certainly is."

Here there was a smart pull at the house-bell that made both of them start.

" *I* started that time," said Mary, laughing a little. "I caught it of you. It is too early for visitors."

However, the drawing-room door was opened by Susan, who announced "Mrs. Hyde." That lady was no favourite with Mary, and she gave an expressive glance at Miss Beaumorice, sweeping her work together at the same time. To her surprise Miss Beaumorice rose in some agitation, and took the initiative, quickly approaching Mrs. Hyde with outstretched hand, and saying,—

"All safe?"

"Yes, all safe," said Mrs. Hyde, laughing, and retaining her hand, while she nodded at Mary, whom she next shook hands with heartily.

"What is this all about?" said Mary, looking mystified, while Miss Beaumorice sat down because she was not quite able to stand.

"Haven't you heard of the railway accident yesterday evening ?" said Mrs. Hyde, rapidly, charmed to have the first use of the subject.

" Margaret's train ?" said Mary, turning very red and then white.

" No, the one before it," said Mrs. Hyde.

" Oh ! thank God," exclaimed Miss Beaumorice.

Mary became extremely agitated, and said, " So *this* was what you were trying to keep from me ?   Do tell me about it."

She became very hysterical, and they had quite enough to do to prevent her from becoming worse.   The usual remedies were tried, old-fashioned and new-fashioned, they telling her all the while that there was actually nothing to be agitated about, since nothing had happened to Margaret.

" Oh, but to think of what *might* have happened !   So near a thing !"   And Mary now yielded to a natural burst of tears, that relieved though they weakened her.

"Yes, when we think of what *might* have happened," said Miss Beaumorice, "it calls on us for very great thankfulness that our good God saw fit to spare us. It pleases Him sometimes just to show us a glimpse of what *might* have befallen us if He had not mercifully withheld it."

"Yes, that's very true," said Mrs. Hyde, who never was guilty of an original observation herself; "and you know it really *did* happen to the other people, poor creatures. Oh! you never knew such a scene. Though more than an hour had passed, some of them were not yet able to be passed on to the hospital, because, you see, the tunnel was choked. Such pools of blood, and—well, we won't dwell on that. We could not go into the waiting-room, you see, because an operation was going on upon the table. And Miss Beaufort saw the arm carried off, and turned so—well, we won't dwell upon that. Your nice young man, Miss Beaumorice, Mr. Ward, is not his name? showed quite a soldier's coolness, and a Christian's humanity too. He had been talking so pleasantly just before; telling us mess-table jokes, and ensigns' squabbles, and about the colour-sergeant that took four or five Russians prisoners, and got promoted to be an officer, and went to a ball given by the sergeants, and saw his wife flirting with her partner, and cried out from the other end of the room, 'Juliana, right about! quick march!' and just when Mr. Ward had got to that, we began to go very slowly, and got slower and slower, and at last came to a complete stop. Then we began to think something was the matter, for the sides of the embankment were heaped with broken-up carriages, and the rails were forced out of place, and a spare engine kept tearing up and down the line as if to clear it of something, and our engine sighed and snorted and groaned like a wild beast very much hurt. Then Mr. Ward put out his head and said, ' Is anything the matter ?' and somebody running along the line answered, ' The tunnel is choked up !' "

CHAPTER IX.

MAKING BAD WORSE.

> "Reasoning at every step he treads,
> Man yet mistakes his way."
>
> COWPER.

"IT must have been fearful," said Mary.

"Oh, beyond description," said Mrs. Hyde. "Three passenger carriages crushed; a great many passengers scalded by steam and boiling water; ten hospital cases, and four deaths. Immense damages will be laid. I shall never go by rail again without insuring myself for a thousand pounds. You may do it, you

know, for a shilling.   One poor old gentleman was scalped as if with a tomahawk,
just like what one reads of in ‘ The Last of
the Mohicans.’   A young lady——”

“ Really,” said Miss Beaumorice, who
saw Mary grow whiter and whiter, “ I
think we had better not dwell on so
painful a subject.   Mrs. Brooke’s nerves
are tender.”

“ Oh, yes, to be sure they are,” said Mrs.
Hyde, scarcely pausing, “ but you know
Miss Beaufort is not hurt.   Mr. Ward saw
her into a cab.   It was getting quite dark,
and I dare say they were uneasy enough
about her at home.   She——”

“ Mary, I think you had better take a
little turn in the garden,” said Miss Beaumorice, “ on the sheltered side.   Susan can
bring you a shawl.   Mrs. Hyde will excuse
you, I know.”

“ Dear me, yes,” said Mrs. Hyde, half
rising, and then sitting down again.

"Perhaps I'd better go. Perhaps you would rather go with her."

"Why, Mr. Brooke left her under my particular care, and she seems rather faint. She is easily overcome just now; and the shock was so unexpected."

"Oh, yes, yes, I can make allowances. Don't think of me, I can finish my visit another time. Don't come to the door with me, pray—I can let myself out. Now I must insist on your remaining with Mrs. Brooke. I thought she would be so glad to hear Miss Beaufort was safe; and Mr. Ward so very polite, I had hardly begun about him, you know. Good-bye; not a step further. I'll finish my visit another time."

"I'm sure I hope she will not," said Mary, when Mrs. Hyde was really gone. "I hope she will not for a long time. I felt all over pins and needles, and so cold! How is it that some people fix you so that you cannot take your eyes off them? I hate people saying, 'Perhaps I'd better go,' *and not going.*"

"You must have a glass of wine now, Mary," said Miss Beaumorice.

"No, my medicine, please, and then I shall like to be a few minutes in the air. What an escape dear Maggie had! how thankful we ought to be!" And a tear shone in her eye.

"She might well say as she did, that she was glad she had lost the first train."

"Oh, yes! I think it quite Providential. Does John know? Have you seen him?"

"He heard of it after leaving you, and looked in on me for a moment, to ask me to come to you and keep you from being frightened, while he went to see how things were."

"It was very good of you to come. Perhaps he is on the line now. I wish he would come back. Has he gone up to town, do you think?"

"I don't know. He might like to do so, knowing I was with you."

Miss Beaumorice wrapped Mary well up, and took her under a sheltered wall, where a few apricots were ripening ; then returned with her, and made her sit down, while she looked over the newspaper. Almost the first paragraph that caught her eye was headed "Frightful Collision in Cowfield Tunnel—three persons killed, eight seriously hurt." It would have alarmed Mary dreadfully had she seen it without being forewarned.

"How quickly they get these things in," said Miss Beaumorice ; "directly anything sensational happens, there always seems a bird in the air to carry word of it to the newspaper office."

"How surprised papa and mamma must have been at Margaret's being so late ! They may only have set it down, though, to my wanting her."

"That would only shift their anxiety from one of you to the other."

"Poor Maggie! And I without the least suspicion or uneasiness about her!"

Mr. Brooke returned soon after luncheon. He had gone to Mr. Beaufort's and seen all the family just before they started for Lowestoft. He had found Margaret writing to Miss Beaumorice as fast as her pen could fly over the paper, to save the post, but he undertook the charge of her letter, so then she wrote a few lines to Mary, suppressing everything sensational, with a reticence Mrs. Hyde would not have appreciated. While they were talking rapidly and rather disjointedly to Mr. Brooke, Alured Ward sent in his card with polite inquiries, and was immediately admitted. His reception was most friendly; he said he was most unwilling to start for the depôt till he had ascertained how Miss Beaufort had got over the fright of the previous evening. They all seemed very glad to see him, hearty words were spoken, and Mr. Beaufort, shaking him warmly by the hand, begged him never in future to consider himself a stranger. Then the general bustle was resumed, for it was time to start for the station, and Alured and Mr. Brooke saw them off; they then shook hands, and took their several ways.

When all this had been related, Mary and Miss Beaumorice ran through Margaret's notes. The first was as follows :—

"MY DEAREST MARY,—

"I shall refer you to Miss Beaumorice for an account of what happened yesterday afternoon, for we are just starting, and John is waiting for my letter. So kind of him to come! I am sure you will be very glad and thankful that I lost the train I had intended to travel in; and besides, I had such a pleasant evening with

Miss Beaumorice; and Mr. Ward unexpectedly dropping in proved a most welcome escort, and there was Mrs. Hyde in the carriage; but, as events turned out, we were both glad to have him, he was so kind and thoughtful. Good-bye now, dearest Mary; take the greatest care of yourself for all our sakes, especially of mine.

"Your loving,

"MARGARET."

To Miss Beaumorice she wrote thus :—

"MY DEAR MISS BEAUMORICE,—

"What a chapter of accidents! You little thought there was anything more before me than a safe and swift journey of an hour, in very pleasant company. We take things too much for granted sometimes. I am sure I did. The first ten miles were indeed very pleasant. I never saw the country look more lovely than with those long, pointed evening shadows *you* taught me to notice and admire; every object looking as if touched up with 'a velvet brush dipped in honey.' Mr. Ward, too, contributed to the pleasure of the journey and amused us very much. All at once, we went very slowly, and then stopped; at first I concluded we had reached another station. When I looked out, however, I saw great heaps of over-turned trucks and shattered railway-carriages lying on the side of the line, and people hurrying to and fro. Mrs. Hyde became frightened directly, and would not be satisfied till Mr. Ward put his head out and called to know what was the matter; for they did not pay the least attention to her. An engine was racing up and down the other line to force a passage through the tunnel. Some one run-ning past told Mr. Ward there had been a collision in it—no lives lost—which was a great mistake. Then we backed to a platform where numbers of people were standing about, looking unhappy or uncomfortable; some of them plastered and bound up. Room for some of these was found in our train. Happening to glance into the window of the waiting-room, which was opened for a minute, I saw what made me feel quite faint — a poor lad on the table had just lost his arm. Luckily we were told afterwards by a gentleman who stepped into our carriage, that it had been under the influence of chloroform; but he sank under the shock to his nervous system nevertheless. Mr. Ward got out for a few minutes. He spoke a few words of comfort to the poor mother; and took down in writing a message to her husband. There was not time for more. When he came back, we were all a good deal solemnized, especially as the gentleman who had joined us had so many sad particulars to give. Mrs. Hyde kept saying, 'Well, I'm sure I'm glad I wasn't in that train.' At last the tunnel was cleared—it was not very pleasant to go through it. We got to town late, and I found papa and mamma in much surprise at the delay, and wondering if Mary were ill. John has just come. Dear Miss Beaumorice, I am so sorry to leave off so abruptly. Mr. Ward has just looked in.

"Your affectionate young friend,
"MARGARET BEAUFORT."

We read of such accidents daily, almost as matters of course, saying, perhaps, 'how dreadful!' or 'what bad management,' and then pass on to the next paragraph. But what a difference it makes if we know one single person involved, or possibly involved, in the catastrophe! Sterne knew this when he worked on the feelings by a single case of captivity instead of a closely packed slave-ship. Margaret had not only been unhurt, but in no danger ; had Mary been well and strong, she would hardly have thought of the collision again, after knowing that her sister was safe. Being already below par, however, made all the difference, and made Miss Beaumorice watchful for her.

She was glad to find, in the course of a day or two, that Mrs. Garrow had called in the interim, and sat some time with Mary, who seemed very much pleased with her visit.

"She is a good old lady," said she. "There is so much heart about her. Good sense, too, and great experience ; she smoothed many of my small anxieties. See what a great book she has sent me ! Too heavy to lift, but I can read it very well on my knee. 'Gilly's Waldenses.' It is not new, but almost seems the fresher for that. Books that come out now are such copies of one another, even in their titles. When you know one, you know all. That has sickened me a good deal of novels. Few original ones come out now, and besides, John does not like my reading many. Still, they take one's thoughts off one's self, sometimes ; but, now that my subscription is up, I don't think I shall renew it. Even a guinea is worth saving, now that a doctor's bill is looming in the distance ; and Mrs. Garrow approved of my saving it, and called it real self-denial. After that, you know, it would be shabby to renew my subscription. She said she would send me some nice books, though I might think them tame at first ; but this is not tame. Dr. Gilly must be old now, for this is dedicated to George the Fourth ! but he must have been young when he started on his tour with two young fresh-men—in December, too. The ascent of

Mont Cenis is very entertaining. Now I have come to Rodolphe Peyrani. What an interesting account it is. How many comforts I have that he was absolutely in need of!"

Miss Beaumorice was not quite like Thomas de Vaux, who feared Cœur de Lion must be dying when he heard him utter a somewhat pious observation; but she was pleased that Mary should have at least begun a kind of reading more beneficial to her. The sacrifice of the subscription would, she was sure, be really an effort to her.

On her return home, she found awaiting her a cheque for her magazine article. What a pleasant surprise! Very good pay, too, she thought; and she resolved to write another essay, nay, several others, directly she had leisure. But how difficult leisure is to command, sometimes! How many little interruptions poke a hole in the frail cobweb—burst the delicate soap-bubble !

Miss Beaumorice's essay was deferred by a succession of trifles. She received another welcome letter from Alured.

" Dear Miss Beaumorice,—

" You may possibly not know that the —th depôt battalion is about to be broken up. The immediate consequence of this decision of the Commander-in-Chief is, that we are under orders to join the head-quarters at Aldershot on the 30th. I shall be very glad of this on some accounts, as I shall see more of the class of men who compose the officers of the service. On the other hand, I shall be sorry to lose sight of the Fleetwood family, and especially of my friend Ainslie, who is going to exchange into another regiment ordered on foreign service. This is out of pure and disinterested friendship for a young fellow whose mother is fast dying of consumption, and who wishes to remain to be a support to her and his sisters. I honour Ainslie for it; it just shows of what stuff he is, for the regiment into which he exchanges is not such a crack one as this. My loss will be nothing to that of Miss Fleetwood's; but her father will allow them to correspond. Ainslie promises to write to me also. Don't I hope he will keep his word? I imagine he writes first-rate letters; but they will not make full amends for our long talks.

"You have doubtless heard of the smash we got into on our way to Charing Cross the other night. Lucky that your charming young friend missed the unlucky train that came to grief. Bad enough as it was —she saw one or two sights that blanched her cheeks. The old lady, whose name I forget, was much more excited; rather clamorous. We got off at last, after awful delay, and as it was late when we reached town, I thought it my duty to inquire for Miss Beaufort next morning. She is now, I hope, enjoying the sea breezes. Mr. Beaufort was extremely polite; begged me not to consider myself a stranger, &c. I shall be most happy to take him at his word, should the opportunity ever offer— but perhaps it never may. I may never see your young friend again. It was happy for me that I dropped in on you that evening.

"Believe me,

"Dear Miss Beaumorice,

"Ever yours affectionately,

"ARTHUR ALURED WARD."

Miss Beaumorice was on her way to the post-office with her acknowledgment of the cheque, when two ladies, who had just left it and were in advance of her, spoke in

such raised voices that it was impossible
not to catch a few words.   These were
they :—

" And she said Miss Beaumorice was
really quite rude to her."

This was certainly rather startling and
unpleasant.   Had Miss Beaumorice been
asked, the moment before, " Have you
reason to suppose that any person in this
place has a case against you ?" she would
unhesitatingly have answered, " Not a creature !"   And yet, the moment the above
words were accidentally heard, something
darted into her head to which she thought
they must have applied, however unjustly.
This was not very comfortable.   Going
into the post-office, she asked for stamps,
and while the postmaster's daughter was
serving her, said quietly—

" Were those the Miss Gambiers who
were here just now ?"

" Yes, ma'am—at least, Miss Gambier and Miss Dawe."

Hum! And who was Miss Dawe? And what concern was it of hers that Miss Beaumorice was thought rude by somebody else? Perhaps it was Mrs. Hyde who had been affronted by her sending Mary into the garden during her visit, but was she wrong in doing it? In another five minutes Mary would have gone off in a dead faint, as she did sometimes, though rarely; and if Miss Beaumorice had not been there as a breakwater, she would have been at Mrs. Hyde's mercy. No, Miss Beaumorice did not, and could not, feel sorry for what she had said, though, perhaps, she might have said it with more circumlocution. Of what value are acquaintance that require circumlocution? Mrs. Hyde herself, too, showed so little of it! So obtuse of her, not to perceive the effect of her shocking stories on Mary! Still, Miss Beaumorice was sorry to lie under the imputation of rudeness.

It was such a pleasure to tell Mrs. Caryl of the cheque.

"And here is the article itself," said Mrs. Caryl, gaily. "See how nice you look, my dear friend! Two copies of the magazine have been sent me—one of them, of course, for you."

"Really this is a very pleasant way of getting money."

"Sometimes—when you have leisure and are in the cue; not if you have to work like a horse in a mill, whether you will or no. Sir Walter Scott well said to his young friend, 'Literature is a good stick, but a bad staff;' a good walking cane, useful and ornamental, but a broken reed to lean with all your weight upon, that will pierce your side. Those lines of Scott's apply so forcibly, I think, to literary success—

> " ' Tell him we play unequal game
>   Whene'er we shoot by Fancy's aim ;
>   That all who on her visions press,
>   Find disappointment dog success,
>   But, missed their wish, lamenting hold
>   Her gilding false for sterling gold.' "

" What a lovely poem Rokeby is !" said Miss Beaumorice. " I hardly know which I enjoy most, the charming descriptions of nature, so perfectly truthful, the unaffected beauty of the moralizing, never forced, or the engaging characters and situations. What can be sweeter than that evening fireside scene, the last ever spent in the old country house, when—

> " ' Two lovers by the maiden sate,
>   Without a glance of jealous hate ;
>   The maid her lovers sat between,
>   With open brow and equal mien ;—
>   It is a sight but rarely spied,
>   Thanks to man's wrath and woman's pride.' "

" Do read me that canto some day when you are in the humour for it."

" I am in the humour now," said Miss

Beaumorice, with alacrity.   And taking down the volume from the shelves, she began the fifth canto—

" 'The sultry summer day is done,' " &c.,

and afterwards talked it over with her friend.   They tried to picture the calm, keen satisfaction it must have given Scott in writing.

In the evening Miss Beaumorice almost involuntarily thought out another little essay, and with a voiceless prayer—

"What in me is dark,
Illumine ; what is low, raise and support,"

which it would be well if every author whispered before dipping pen in ink, she wrote the rough draft with facility, leaving revision for the morrow.

As about this time there was a lull in her life, she watched the fluctuations of her friend's health, gardened in the long evenings, assisted by her maids, answered letters, and did much needlework. She passed hours in reading during the sultry afternoons, when it was too hot to go out. Almost too hot to write also, but where there's a will there's a way. Her second essay was thought over, revised, copied, and sent off. She was in no hurry to write another immediately.

One day she went to the draper's for some trifling purchase, when she saw Mrs. Hyde in the shop, whom she had not seen for some time. Mrs. Hyde bowed coldly enough, and renewed a dialogue with a shopwoman about some lace she wished to match, but the remainder of which had, unfortunately, been disposed of. Mrs. Hyde was inclining to make a grievance of it, when Miss Beaumorice, glancing at the pattern on the counter, said cordially—

"I think I can assist you, Mrs. Hyde.

I bought the remnant, but have not yet used it. Another pattern will suit me equally well."

Mrs. Hyde was instantly all complacence. She could hardly make sure that Miss Beaumorice meant to be taken at her word, till again assured of it. Miss Beaumorice bought another lace, and promised to send Mrs. Hyde the remnant on her return home. But this Mrs. Hyde would by no means allow; she insisted on returning with Miss Beaumorice to fetch it herself, talked all the way, paid a lengthened visit, inquired particularly after Mrs. Brooke, learnt from Miss Beaumorice that her mother had been consumptive, which accounted for what might have appeared undue anxiety about her, went away in the best of humours, and finished by calling on Miss Gambier and telling her how excessively friendly Miss Beaumorice had been in letting her have the lace which she would not otherwise have matched. The kind word and kind deed had removed the little heart-burning.

CHAPTER X.

A PUZZLER.

" Oh, teach him, while your lessons last,
To guide the present by the past."

Rokeby.

ONE day, Alured forwarded a note to Miss Beaumorice from his father, which he had received inclosed in one to himself. It puzzled her a good deal. Why he should write to her at all was a question, and what he wrote was hardly easier to understand. First he thanked her for his boy's successful examination, which annoyed her, as she knew it had not been in any way owing to herself,

but Miss Partridge; she had not even coun-
selled the suppression of truth about his
illness, which Dr. Ward had urged. After
this, he alluded darkly to projects which
were hereafter to have magnificent results;
but broke off from disclosing them with
" Enough — You shall know more hereafter." More? why, she knew nothing!
What was the good of hinting at things
mysteriously, and not speaking out? He
had better have said nothing: there was
no sense in such a letter. Then she remembered a trait of Dr. Ward's character
of old, which in earlier days she had not
liked to notice; viz. a love of mystery, and
of talking grand, and exciting curiosity
which was generally disappointed. She
added this trait to the rest. One thing
she liked in him—he was undeniably fond
of his boy.

Alured had told her at Easter, that papa
was by no means so rich as was thought,

and that the castle and his pension from the Prince were nearly all he had, after the Countess's death. Idalia's being portionless had induced him to place her in the Moravian school, though rather too old for it. Did Miss Beaumorice think with more indifference of Dr. Ward because he was poor? Far from it; that would be a great deal more likely to interest her in him. But somehow, she had not much interest in him now, rich or poor; she had so long felt their characters and paths were different.

In Alured she always took lively interest; and his letter to her, inclosing his father's, gave her the usual pleasure. He said:

"The parting is over, dear Miss Beaumorice! Ainslie has sailed for Canada. If my loss is great, what must be Miss Fleetwood's? but she bears it nobly and with her usual gentleness, though I think it wears her a good deal. He commended her to my brotherly kindness, and as long as I am within reach, you may depend on my showing it. It seems the only thing I can do now for Ainslie. I verily believe we love each other like brothers. A few of the subs. thought it witty to call us ' the sweethearts,' till they found Ainslie had a real one. That gave him dignity in the eyes of the unfortunates who hadn't one, and they let him alone. I believe friends and married couples don't suit the worse for being diverse though not opposite. Certainly something drew Ainslie and me together, though we were so different—he deep, I shallow, he steady, I impatient, he caring little for the opinion of the world when he knew he was right, I guided a good deal by it. He will be sure to do well, go where he will, but he will probably not be popular in any mess ; his high principles will make him lonely, though kind and obliging to all. God's blessing be with him! This is said with the seriousness of a prayer. Before he went, he got me to promise I would read a chapter of the New Testament every evening, at the same hour with himself. This I am faithfully doing. It will give you a little idea of the stamp of man he is; of the kind of influence he exerts. Miss Fleetwood reads at the same time with him, morning as well as evening. Surely the promise 'where two or three are gathered together,' &c., may be hoped for in this instance.

"Since you like knowing what I do, here it is from the beginning. My servant calls me at half-past six, and takes my clothes to brush while I have my bath. I then exercise (without dumb bells) finish my toilette and breakfast in the mess-room along with the others, who chiefly read the papers in silence. After breakfast

I proceed to the barracks, see the pay issued to the men by the colour-serjeant, who keeps the accounts of the company, and return to my quarters for a quarter of an hour; then walk down to the drill-shed, and join a class which is questioned on military matters by the adjutant. This lasts an hour and a half.

" Then we have an hour's drill; and, being dismissed, return to the officers' quarters. I go to the reading-room and begin a letter to Ainslie. Then lunch, which I make my dinner, intending to drink tea with the Fleetwoods. After lunch, I read up some drill, with the help of Potts' 'Drill Models,' for about an hour; then put on mufti and enjoy a waking dream (or perhaps *not* waking) in my portable bed chair. Then to my friends, whose companionship I hope you think I have earned.

" Miss Beaufort wouldn't think so perhaps. Young ladies are not so indulgent as ladies of a riper age. You and Miss Partridge are never hard upon a poor fellow. I wonder when the next war will be, and where. The French seem making wonderful preparations for a scrimmage somewhere ; not with us perhaps, but the Emperor does not generally reveal his intentions long beforehand. They say he must fight with somebody to give the people something to think of.

"'Who o'er the herd would wish to reign?'

"I hope you are quite well.
"Affectionately yours,
"A. A. WARD,"

"P.S.—Just returned from the Fleetwood's. A sorrowful visit. Ainslie's departure of course depresses all; besides which a low fever has broken out in the village, and not only has Miss Fleetwood visited the sick, but her youngest brother is now laid up at home with it, and she is constantly with him. Her father is full of anxiety on her account, her constitution being so delicate.

"I'll let you know soon how she is. I'm sure you'll wish to know."

Indeed she wished it; for she loved all this group of young people. She anxiously awaited news.

It came at length; from Aldershot. Some days had passed. The letter was sealed with black.

"Ellen is dead! O, sorrowful news! I have only learnt the bare fact, and that is bad enough. I have written a few lines to Ainslie, and will write again by the next mail. Dear lassie! she has left some sorrowful hearts behind her. I am in blank fear of the blow which this will strike on Ainslie. Thousands of miles from sympathy—with her lying cold in the grave—it would drive me mad.

"For her I cannot regret it. For Ainslie I do principally, though I am sure it will do him good in the end. He used to hate the thoughts of her being touched by sin and pain and sorrow—and now she is safe from all. And when we see her again, she will be a perfect creature indeed.

"We could not expect to keep her long—she was too good for this world—we shall go to her, but she will not return to us. And if she is taken, that Ainslie's aims and purposes may thereby be steadied and strengthened, who shall say that this will not prove a blessed event in the end? I trust that he will, after the first burst of grief, remember that there is no such thing as death for *her*—only transition.

"The last time I saw them together was on the railway platform. They were going down to spend a few hours with his mother, who wished to know Ellen; and Ainslie wanted me to go too; but, being a total stranger, I thought it best not to do so. We parted at London Bridge station, after sitting together for a quarter of an hour building castles in the air as to what we would do when Ainslie should return in two years' time. Then I saw them into the train, and wished them good-bye. Little I thought it was to be my last sight of them together in this world.

"Do you know when the Canadian mails go out? I'm half in hope that my letter to Ainslie may have gone out in the same mail as the news. It seems so hard that one can't give him warning—not the slightest—of the blow which is coming.

"I have been thinking a good deal of the happy times we used to spend together, both before I had the slightest idea of his engagement and afterwards. Instead of weeks, I fancy it months. Afterwards, the house was almost like a home to me. Of course I was nothing to her when Ainslie was by, nor at any other time, but as his friend; but I used to like talking to her. I remember our talks at twilight when we were all together, and her assenting so cordially to what Ainslie said of its being better to die in harness than to drag out an idle life—to die in a good cause than to lengthen life at the price of allowing old abuses and evils to go unremedied. *She* has died in a good cause, surely—acting a mother's part to a little motherless brother.

"Good-bye once more. Do you believe in apparitions? presentiments? forewarnings? Soldiers do, a good many of them."

Miss Beaumorice cried over this letter. Then she wrote such an answer as only a woman could write, a woman who had felt

and suffered, and seen loved ones suffer.
In the course of her answer she quoted the
following lines of Fanny Kemble's, and remarked what noble principles of action
they gave :—

> " What shall I do with all the days and hours
>   That must be counted ere I see thy face ?
> How shall I charm the interval that lours
>   Between this time and that sweet time of grace ?
>
> " Shall love for thee lay in my soul the sin
>   Of casting from me God's great gift of time ?
> Shall I, these mists of memory locked within,
>   Leave and forget life's purposes sublime ?
>
> " Oh ! how or by what means shall I contrive
>   To bring the hour that re-unites us near ?
> How may I teach my drooping heart to live
>   Until the blessed time when thou art here ?
>
> " I'll tell thee : for thy sake I will lay hold
>   Of all good aims, and consecrate to thee
> In worthy deeds each moment that is told,
>   While thou, beloved one ! art far from me.
>
> " For thee I will arouse my thoughts to try
>   All heavenward flights, all high and holy strains,
> For thy dear sake I will wait patiently
>   Through these long hours, nor call their minutes
>   pains.

> "I will this dreary blank of absence make
>   A noble task-time, and will therein strive
> To follow excellence, and to o'ertake
>   More good than I have won ; since yet I live.
>
> "So may this fated time build up in me
>   A thousand graces which shall thus be thine :
> So may my love and longing hallowed be,
>   And thy dear thought an influence divine."

Miss Beaumorice only meant at first to copy a verse or two of the above (rather shortened even now), but as she proceeded, their uncommon beauty and wisdom made her write them all out, even at the risk of taxing Alured's patience, for her aim always was

> "The mind to strengthen and anneal,
>   While on the stithy glowed the steel."

Her reward was the following answer :—

> "C Lines, Aldershot,
> "July 13.

"I have been a little worried by looking over the company's monthly accounts and so forth, so that I have not been able, dear Miss Beaumorice, to answer your letter as soon as I should. I inclose a long letter from Ainslie, hastily written on the voyage out, and wound up after. They had marched twenty miles to quarters, he carrying the colours, as junior ensign. Poor fellow! he will be in great grief just now. He knew nothing of it, of course, when he wrote. It is satisfactory that he carries his flag so pluckily. He has immense muscular strength—it is one of the things I rather envy him. But we all have what is best for us. I write to him weekly, giving him an hour every Sunday evening. Please return the letter. I keep most letters docketted, and with dates, so that many years hence I may see what my friends were like in my young days.

"I think it only right to tell you that my answer to Ainslie's question about lotteries and sweepstakes, though the same in fact as yours would have been, was in principle different. His question is, 'Do you mean to put in for these things?' My answer is, 'No, and I am glad you do not; simply because I have no money to throw away, nor, I imagine, have you.' You would have taken higher ground; but in the first place, I knew it to be unnecessary, and in the next, I don't like to say hard things of other men. You know already what my practice is. I do not choose to set a bad example, nor to follow a multitude to do evil. Exceedingly as I should object to losing, I should equally hate winning my neighbour's money; therefore it would be positively absurd as well as wrong in me to bet.

"Mrs Butler's verses on 'Absence' are admirably to the point at present, I think. I shall copy them for Ainslie. I inclose you a hymn that George Fleetwood has copied for me, and I for Ainslie, from dear Ellen's common-place book. If Ainslie will only, through Divine help, meet his grief in that manner, it will prove a blessing to him."

The lines were those beginning—

"Father, I know that all my life
   Is portioned out for me,
And the changes which are sure to come,
   I do not fear to see ;
But I ask Thee for a present mind
   Intent on following Thee."

Miss Beaumorice knew them well already, but she was pleased that one young man should copy them for another, who copied them for a third, and all of a profession not supposed to be too serious. It reminded her of the " three-fold cord not quickly broken."

She took the lines to show Mary, who said with a kind of good-humoured reproof :—

"Why, how long it is since you came near me! Almost a week. But I don't mean to complain seriously, for you give me a large portion of your time; only there is no one I like to see so much. Mrs. Garrow, too, pays me nice long visits. See, she has cut out these little garments, and shown me how to put them together. I am to have a lending basket, so I shall not be altogether useless. She told me a piece of news too. Margaret was not out, after all! Mr. Frank Garrow and Grace Nuneham *are* engaged, only nothing is to be said about it at present."

"Margaret was sure they cared for one another, but I did not encourage her to think so, because I thought there was nothing in it."

"You made her a little ashamed even of speaking of it to me, and I took your view of it, as she *is* rather fanciful sometimes; and I thought she might better employ her mind. However, Mrs. Garrow looks on it as a real attachment, and a satisfactory one, too; she says the Nunehams are all so well brought up. She would have preferred Caroline if she had not been perhaps rather too old. Grace is not quite twenty. Besides, Mr. Nuneham could not have spared Caroline without the greatest inconvenience, so it is well that Grace is the one preferred. They must wait till Mr. Garrow has a living, or at least a curacy, but they don't seem to mind that. Mrs. Garrow thinks it will do them good. *I* know that people may be very happy on a curacy."

"I don't think you have a drawback, except delicate health."

"And we must all have something."

"Ah, we must, indeed." And Miss Beaumorice told her the little tale of sorrow she had recently received from Alured, and ended by showing her the verses.

Mary was touched, and said, "I shall like to copy them, if you will let me. They will do just as well for me as for Miss Fleetwood."

"Oh, yes."

"How people are mistaken in young officers! They think them all so foolish!"

"Perhaps most of them are. Alured has complained of their frivolous talk at the mess-table. But perhaps they would have been equally empty anywhere else, only not so noticeable as when they are herded together. When the majority are foolish and rattling, it requires extra steadiness in a high-minded young man to keep his ground without offending, or, if need be, even at the price of offending."

"Mr. Ainslie seems of that sort."

" And this sad loss will make him more so than ever. It will even make it easier to him to be so, ' to carry his flag pluckily,' as Alured says, for a time at any rate. Not for long, perhaps.

> " ' Why, soldiers, why
>   Should we be melancholy, boys ?
>   Why, soldiers, why,
>   Whose business is to die ?'

That is the burthen of their song, commonly. And what a burthen it is !—unless taken in a very different sense indeed from the obvious one. *Then* it would suit the cheerful, heroic Christian. Do you remember the death of Captain Mercer ? A shot struck him in the face and carried away part of his jaw—he lay on the field all night—no one could rescue him. In the morning the Maories surrendered, and he was brought in. His poor wife travelled forty miles to come to him. Though he could not speak to her, his composure was perfect. He wrote to her in pencil, 'My darling, do not grieve—I have peace, deep, deep as a river!'"

"What a mind he must have had!"

"His life must have been a training for his death."

Mary was silent a little while, and presently said,—

"Miss Beaumorice, I should not like Margaret to marry a soldier."

"Oh no, a clergyman will be better," said Miss Beaumorice, smiling a little.

"Or a merchant, or banker, or country gentleman—anything, I think, but a soldier."

"These things are generally arranged by the parties principally concerned. Interference does not usually have much effect, or if it has, it is not always with good result. A year ago, I don't think you had any special partiality for a country curacy."

"Oh yes, I had."

" Had you ? I did not know it. I knew you so little, it seems, that at first I was distrustful of your taking to your duties kindly."

" I like them now, though I can fulfil so few. I believe I set off on rather a wrong principle. I thought I would have a few pleasant months first, and settle down to work afterwards."

" Such as dinner-parties, morning visits, and so on, without thinking of their effect on the poorer classes."

" Perhaps it was a good thing that my first dinner was such a failure. How Dr. and Mrs. Garrow must have laughed in their hearts ! If they did not, they must have been very good-natured—and that's what they are. I like Mrs. Garrow more and more. As for visitors, Alicia cured me of wanting any more to stay in the house. Perhaps, when I'm quite well and strong again, I may like to have Laura Field and

Cecilia Nash; but I don't know. I care more for Margaret now than for any one else."

"She is a dear good girl. Well, you have a piece of news for her; though perhaps she will say it is no news."

"She will be elated at having been in the right after all. She took great interest in the Nunehams, and I thought them very nice friends for her; so safe! If girls must have ardent friendships, it is so important they should be good ones. Margaret has no very nice friends in town; she seems very fond, just now, of supplying the governess's place to the children. Mamma saw no need to take Miss Davis to Lowestoft, and she herself was glad of a holiday, so it was arranged that Margaret should teach the children for the time, and she likes doing so very well—very much, I should say; more than I should. They are very fond, now, of hunting for shells.

Do you know of any nice little book on conchology ?"

"Yes, I have one or two. I will send them to her by book post."

"Thank you very much. That poor woman Mrs. Garrow took me to see, is dead at last."

"Which poor woman ?"

"The one I said had a skin like wash-leather. Mrs. Garrow was with her. She said she seemed in heaven even while yet on earth. She seemed as if she saw something or some one, and said, in a kind of rapture, ' Don't you see ? Don't you see ?' Those were her last words."

"I have heard of such cases. They are very impressive."

"You don't think it was delirium ?"

"No."

"Do you think it was what is called ' the beatific vision ?' "

"I think so."

" One would like to have it when dying," said Mary after a pause. " I do not shrink now, from the subject of death; there is something very beautiful in it, though very awful. I used to dislike John's going to visit the dying, though I knew it was his duty, but I do not mind it now; I ask him about it afterwards. On Sunday evening I sent Susan to church, and only kept Jem with me. I asked him what he was reading. He said, ' Jessica's First Prayer.' I told him he might read it to me; so he did, and very well, too. It made me cry, and towards the end, his voice quavered, and I thought he was going to cry too. Just then, to my surprise, they came back from church. He said, ' How quickly the time has passed !' "

CHAPTER XI.

ALL IN THE DAY'S WORK.

"Coming events cast their shadows before."
CAMPBELL.

T is impossible to say how long Frank Garrow's engagement to Grace Nuneham might have been kept quiet, had it not transpired to Mrs. Hyde, who immediately told of it to the Miss Gambiers. They never kept any secrets, though they were exceedingly fond of finding them out, so that they were sure to spread it to others till the news became stale even to themselves.

The happiness of the Nuneham family

was certainly increased by the engagement. They were not at all characterized by ambition or day-dreaming; they took deep interest in one another; and the happiness of one of them was the happiness of all. They had the greatest esteem and respect for Dr. and Mrs. Garrow, and the greatest liking for their nephew; so that having a kind of property in him was a delightful event. Mr. Nuneham's satisfaction was still deeper and accompanied with more thankfulness than he found words to express.

Mrs. Garrow seemed more genial and expansive than ever when Miss Beaumorice called on her, and frankly spoke on the subject.

"Of course Frank might have done better, in a worldly sense, if he had been inclined;" said she, "but you know we are not worldly people. It would be inconsistent enough for Dr. Garrow to preach as he does, week after week, on 'Love not the world,' and similar texts, and then act in opposition to them. That is not what *he* calls Christianity; and Frank has not been caught by a pretty face, though Grace is nice-looking enough, everybody must allow; but she has more than her looks to boast of. Those girls have such rectitude: such simplicity and innocence—every cardinal virtue, I think! If you want to find complete contrasts to the modern fast young ladies, you have only to look at the Nunehams.

"And such managers," she presently added. "If Grace does not bring a fortune, she will save one. No high-flying ideas: if a dress is not worn out, she will never think of being tired of it, or fancy others tired of seeing her in it. If she sees some one else in a pretty silk, she will not begin immediately to hanker for one like it. If she comes to dine with us, she will not—ah well, a good deal depends on bringing up, and the Nunehams have all been brought up well."

One day Miss Beaumorice found Mary resting on the sofa, but looking fresher and brighter than usual.

"Only think of Mrs. Garrow's kindness," said she. "She came here in her close carriage on purpose to tempt me to a drive. Of course I was very glad to go, and she took me all round Earl's Forest and the Abbey Grange, and insisted on having the glasses up all the time. It was very good of her, and I feel all the better for it."

This did not prove a solitary instance of Mrs. Garrow's kindness. She took Mary three or four drives; and also tried to persuade Mrs. Caryl to go out with her; but Mrs. Caryl was not equal to this. Indeed it was one of her trials, that even considerate friends did not know how little she was equal to. Her niece Edith continually wrote how sure she was that if she could be transported to the south of France, where she and her father now were, it would give her a new lease of life ! And others who had really been most kind in their little proofs of sympathetic attention, thought Mrs. Caryl had now turned the corner and was doing as well as could be expected. Perhaps so, but only Miss Beaumorice and Mrs. Garrow knew what that amounted to.

With a kind of quiet desperation, she went on correcting her proofs till they were finished. "It can only give me a little more pain," she thought, "and I will not leave anything incomplete behind me if I can help it. If I must cry, I will do something worth crying for. Besides, I am too old for a cry-baby."

Again Mary, after progressing so nicely, lost all the ground she had gained. Miss Beaumorice found her in tears about it.

"You must not think I am giving way," she said, looking rather ashamed, "only it does seem too disappointing. If ill-health is to be my trial, I must submit to it; only this way of losing it,—by such trifling things as a current of air and an open carriage-glass—"

"You must remember, dear Mary, who said 'I am the way.' If we chose our own ways, they would hardly be trials at all."

Afterwards Mrs. Garrow met Miss Beaumorice, and said—

"I want to speak to you about our little friend. I am so sorry she has lost ground again! That east wind yesterday! She *would* have the glass down on that side, on my account, I am sure, though she said she liked it. Mr. Finch looked in on me just now. I asked him what he thought of her. He said he wished she could winter in the south of France. Do you think she would like it, if it were practicable?"

"For both of them? Yes, very much; but it hardly is so, I suppose."

"Oh, I was not making a question of that."

Miss Beaumorice, on her return home, found a letter awaiting her which had come by the twelve o'clock post. It was from Dr. Ward; and she opened it with a little impatience, saying inwardly, "Why should he write?"

Why, indeed? The letter did not solve the mystery, but it spoke of the surprise he concluded it would give her, "let him hope, not altogether unmingled with pleasure," to learn that her old, and, he might say, affectionate friend, was on his way to England for a rapid visit, which, however, he meant to include a still shorter visit to herself. Important affairs, &c. . . . The words danced before her eyes without conveying meaning. She stood in blank surprise; she felt she did not want to see him. Wild ideas of escaping somewhere,—of going to stay with Mrs. Caryl, or with her uncle—presented themselves, only to be regretfully pronounced out of the question. She must remain at her post, at her visitor's mercy. "Surely, an Englishman's house is his castle! and, therefore, an Englishwoman's is *hers*."

Dr. Ward's house was a castle; his letter was dated from it, but at the foot of the page was a hardly legible postscript, hastily announcing himself already arrived in England, so that he hoped to have the great pleasure of seeing her soon after her reception of his letter.

Her consternation was great. " He might have given me the option of declining a visit, instead of taking it for granted in this way that I should be glad to receive it! Why am I not glad? Ought I to be? Need I be? Why am I so much put out about it? I am not young now— young?—No, indeed! nor can he be. He must be as many years older than I am as he ever was, and that must make him— dear me, when I have thought of him at all, he has always seemed almost stationary. The knowledge of Alured's age might have prevented that. He seems very fond of Alured, and Alured certainly is of him. How tiresome that he could not have written sooner, and said by what train he should come. It seems as if done on purpose to pre-occupy my whole time with uncertainty. (She gave an impatient 'tut'). He may be here by the very next train. That will be due in half an hour. I must dress, I suppose, and have wine and cake. No need for him to lunch at my dinner— certainly not. I know my own meaning, and I do *not* mean to be on anything like terms of familiar intimacy again. That sherry has not been very freshly decanted; I had better have a fresh bottle, I believe. Men think so much of these things—he

always did. The old sherry—my father's—
of which there is so little left."

Hardening herself in this way, Miss
Beaumorice gave the necessary directions
and went to dress. Not one pin, one bow,
would she have for smartness ; not one ring,
one brooch, one chain. A loud ring at the
visitors' bell made her start violently, but
she told herself, " That cannot be him."

Jessy, flurried, as if sympathetically, presented herself the next moment, with a
card. " Dr. Ward." For an instant, Miss
Beaumorice flushed deep red. She would
not go down till the flush had subsided ; and
yet it was unbearable that he should mis-
interpret or truly interpret the reason of
the delay. She put force on herself, and
went downstairs at her usual pace. Her
step was neither so quick nor so light as it
had been. She opened the drawing-room
door.

" Miss Beaumorice !"

Dr. Ward had stepped quickly forward, taken her hand and kissed it before she could draw breath. He retained it as she walked to her seat and then ensued a few commonplaces which neither of them succeeded in making very coherent. Her head was in a maze, but she did not show perturbation outwardly. She would have been thankful to know how well and composedly she played her part—just interested enough in the visit of an old friend, the husband of Louisa, the father of Alured—and nothing more.

Dr. Ward was a good deal more—and there was a good deal more of him. He was always tall and rather commanding in person and carriage—he had now grown large, and looked considerably older than Miss Beaumorice had pictured him—still handsome, or what most people would term so, but with something that Miss Beaumorice had never allowed herself to see before, showy, made-up, studied, not of the highest school of refinement, which is simple. His dress, too, was showy and somewhat foreign ; at least, that was the excuse Miss Beaumorice made for the rings, and the pin, and the guard, and the studs, and the gold-mounted double eye-glass, all taken in by her at a glance. Soon he was talking to her of his delight at seeing her looking so well— as well as ever! *was* she not so? he trusted she was, he hoped she had a long future of health and happiness before her. He——

Enter Jessy with wine and cake. (That will be a signal, thought Miss Beaumorice, that nothing more will be forthcoming.) He waved them off ; and at a sign from Miss Beaumorice, Jessy placed them on the table and retreated. Her entrance had checked Dr. Ward's fluency and fervour. He was thrown out, as if he had conned his part by rote and dropped the thread.

To prevent an awkward pause, Miss Beaumorice inquired if he had seen Alured. That started him off again, but not in the intended direction. No, he had not seen him yet—impulse made him run down to her first—and how much he had to thank her for!—and that good Miss Partridge—with regard to Alured! They had made a man of him; given him aims and resolutions. In fact, it was all *her* doing, for he had only known Miss Partridge through her.

Miss Beaumorice spoke a few words of hearty praise of Alured and Miss Partridge.

He could take it all on her word; he was sure Miss Partridge was one of the excellent of the earth; a charming woman. And now, to enter on a subject nearer home—nearer the heart—(Miss Beaumorice trembled for the next word, but without need). She knew—his boy must have told her—what a fine old Schloss he had on the Rhine ?

" Oh yes."

——Which required immense keeping up ; but, since the poor Countess's death, he had no longer had means or use for it. One evening, as he paced the lonely halls, a prey to dejection, a thought, an inspiration had come to him seeming to show an opening from all his difficulties, to usefulness, cheerfulness, and fortune !

Miss Beaumorice became all attention. She knew how devotedly he had always loved his profession and his fellow creatures. What if he were to convert his spacious edifice into a Sanatorium for consumptive and rheumatic patients, replete with every luxury, elegance, and amusement—baths, galleries, music-rooms, billiard-rooms, croquet-grounds, conservatories, &c., &c.

Miss Beaumorice was immensely relieved, and even amused at herself for having been in alarm. He caught the quickened intelligence in her eye, saw her pleased, and became quite eloquent in his details, even worthy of a once eminent auctioneer, Mr. George Robins! She was going to avail herself of the first pause, to congratulate him on his project and wish him entire success, but that pause was not, even for a moment, afforded. What could a poor bereaved widower do at the head of such an establishment without a *placens uxor* to share his weal and his responsibility? to charm all around her with her cheerfulness, sweetness, and *savoir faire?* to soothe the suffering, enliven the low-spirited, reassure anxious relatives at a distance, do the honours as only a graceful, highly-educated English lady could — be the delight of the circle, the life of the castle, the better half in every sense, of its grateful master? Would Miss Beaumorice be that woman?

Dr. Ward was so possessed with the conviction that he had only to ask and obtain, that as soon as modest dignity permitted, she would answer in the affirmative,—that she had to say no many times and in many forms before he could believe her in earnest. He was very much hurt when he found she really meant it; he expostulated, recapitulated, urged, entreated, made a very good case, and pleaded it very well too; but all in vain. Then he paused, gave a great sigh, and seemed hardly able to realize his failure; the destruction of his castle in the air. " You would be the very person," he repeated, with great regret, " you would be the very person!"

Miss Beaumorice really pitied him, but not to the point of letting her good nature entirely overthrow all her own views and wishes. When he fully perceived this, he was too well bred to push the question any further, and made as though he were about to go. It ended, however, in his going all over again a great deal of his project, independent of any reference to herself, which when he did, she took real interest in it. He pulled out plans, and photographs, and estimates, and rough drafts of prospectuses, and asked her advice and opinion, which, as far as she could, she willingly gave, though saying it was worth little, as she had no experience.

" Oh, but you have such a mind !" which she had no mind to argue one way or the other. In short, they talked themselves and each other into perfect good humour before the close of this curious interview ; and when he really went away, it was with a prolonged and tender pressure of the hand and assurance of unalterable regard.

When he was actually gone, she drew

a long, deep breath. She felt greatly fatigued in body and mind ; just as people sometimes do when they "think they want a glass of wine."

That was not her restorative. It was considerably past her usual dinner-hour, but she felt neither hunger nor thirst. She was surprised when Jessy came in to say dinner was on table, and was ready to desire the table might be cleared, but thought it best to sit down to it, to save appearances. She ate without knowing what she was eating, and as soon as dinner was over, she settled herself in her easy chair and fell into a deep reconsideration of all that had passed. The result was a feeling of intense relief that she had not been talked into a different decision.

The whole story of her life rose vividly before her ; she seemed hardly the same person. How many things had given her grief and pain that had issued in good! How much that had annoyed and tormented her she could now remember with indifference! Some who had appeared objects of envy, she had since learnt to regard with pity; others whom she had estimated highly had fallen sadly short of the mark—in a word, she had fresh reason to repeat

> "There's a Divinity that shapes our ends,
> Rough hew them how we will."

Miss Beaumorice could not settle heartily to anything that afternoon. That it might not be wholly profitless, she cut out some household work for her maids and sat down to a goodly portion of it herself. Her fingers were busy, and her thoughts were busy too, but gradually became quieter. The evening post brought her a proof of her second essay. What a refreshment it was to read it! How completely it changed the current of her thoughts! By bedtime the irritation of her nerves was quite allayed, and she slept peacefully.

The next few days were spent at home, where there was work to be done by workmen that required supervision. When she next visited Mary, she had another surprise; it seemed a week of surprises, yet this was only the second.

"Miss Beaumorice, only think of what has happened! John has the offer of a foreign chaplaincy for a twelvemonth."

"My dear Mary, the very thing of all others for you. Is he going to accept it?"

"Yes, I think so, if everything can be arranged."

"You like the idea, do not you?"

"Very much. The south of France, you know. At Cannes."

"What will the Garrows say?"

"It has been offered through them."

" How very satisfactory ! How soon are you to start ?"

" In a fortnight. A few letters must be exchanged first."

" And Dr. Garrow must find a new curate, I suppose."

" Mr. Frank Garrow has offered. You know he wants a title for orders. He will take this house just as he finds it."

" That will save you anxiety. How well everything has been arranged."

" Just like Mrs. Garrow. I cannot express how obliged to her I am."

" You must let me help you to pack."

" Thank you, but I am sure Margaret will come if she can."

" I shall miss you, Mary."

" And I shall miss you, dear Miss Beaumorice. You have been such a very kind friend to me. I must not expect to find such friends as you and Mrs. Garrow anywhere else."

"I hope you will. Dear me, how strange it seems. I can hardly realize it. Does Mr. Brooke like it?"

"Oh, immensely! though he was growing very fond of his work here, and rather proud of Dr. Garrow's approval. Do you know much about Cannes?"

"I ought to do so, for I have read Miss Brewster's account of it more than once. I must look it up."

"Let me see it, please."

"I know she says that many bronchial affections are cured there, and that the air exhilarated her like champagne."

"Delightful! I feel as if it must make me well."

"I trust it will; but you must beware of over-fatiguing yourself with long walks however strong you may feel at the time; and always be provided with a shawl to protect you from the sudden changes of temperature. Especially protect your head from the sun, and have a thick veil, a wide hat lined with white paper, and a white umbrella !"

CHAPTER XII.

BETTER FORTUNE ELSEWHERE.

> " Our little lives are kept in equipoise
> By opposite attractions and desires,
> The struggle of the instinct that enjoys,
> And the more noble instinct that aspires."
>   LONGFELLOW.

MARY seemed to grow fonder of her home and neighbours now that she was going to leave them, but would have been terribly disappointed had anything prevented it. The excitement seemed to do her good, and though at times she flagged, it was only with—

> " That feeling of sadness and longing
> Which is not akin to pain,
> And resembles sorrow only
> As the mist resembles rain."

Margaret joyfully accepted the invitation as soon as she received it, and had permission, if Mary liked it, to accompany her on the journey, and stay with her through the winter; Mr. Beaufort undertaking the additional expense. Mary gladly closed with this offer, which was equally agreeable to Mr. Brooke.

Miss Beaumorice thought Mr. Brooke came out strongly, under the prospect of a new field of action, which, after all, did not threaten to be a very heavy one. He told Miss Beaumorice with a smile, that Dr. Garrow was taking the opportunity to peg into him pretty vigorously with what he ought to do, and pray for, and set his face against, in a Romanist country.

"'My dear Brooke,' he says, (in that paternal way of his), 'you must not come back a pervert, or I can't take you on again, you know. It's all very well for you to express gratitude on account of your wife, but that would be a very poor way of showing it. So for goodness sake, don't give heed to fables and traditions, which minister questions rather than godly edifying. The end of the commandment, you know, is charity out of a pure heart, and a good conscience and faith unfeigned. So, what old St. Paul said to his young minister, Timothy, I say to you—" So do ;" or *do so,* if you like it better—it comes to the same thing. Remember that some, having put these away, have made shipwreck. " Thou knowest how to behave in the house of God : take heed, therefore, unto thyself and unto thy doctrine—*continue* in them ; for in thus doing, thou shalt both save thyself and them that hear thee." ' And really, Miss Beaumorice, it was well said of the good old gentleman."

The fortnight ran its course quickly. Margaret was in full activity, helping Mary to pack, going round to pay bills, execute small errands, and take kind farewells and little presents to the poor people, and yet finding time for walks and talks with Miss Beaumorice and the Nunehams.

Miss Beaumorice was not long without another letter from Alured. He wrote :—

> " C Lines,
> " Sept. 3.

" What a treat I have had, dear Miss Beaumorice, in this visit from my father ! So well, too, as he is looking ! Don't you think he looks younger every year ? I forgot you had not seen him for many years, but I think you would hardly find him much altered. I am glad he ran down to you. He told you, he said, all about his new project. A capital one, is not it ? He said it encouraged him so, that you heartily approved of it. I know he always relies on your sympathy and judgment. A use is found now, or soon will be, for the thirty-six bedrooms! His head is full of uphol-stery and so forth. Advertisements are already being struck off, with photographic head-pieces; I'll send you a few of them. Miss Partridge is delighted. By-the-bye, I forgot I had not told you of our seeing her; but I daresay she has. My father was determined on it; he thought I owed her so much, and that he owed her a father's thanks. She was looking so well, and was so much pleased with him. At first, he only sent in our cards, but she came out of the morning-room, all smiles, and would make us come in. The old Countess of Tilbury happened to be with her; she depends a good deal on Miss Partridge's attention, now the younger countess is away, and she was quite taken with my father—women always are, I think. When she found he was the prince's physician, she told him all her complaints, which he listened to with the greatest interest, and told her he knew exactly what would be good for her—*regimen;* in addition to which, he would give her a prescription, which he did.

" After this he got upon the *grand subject* of the Sanatorium, which the Countess and Miss Partridge listened to with the greatest interest; and the Countess said if there should be anything to subscribe, she should be most happy; and at any rate he might rely on her recommendation. So my father came away delighted. He has a few affairs to settle, and is as busy as a bee, and as blythe as a schoolboy during the holidays; but he will soon leave England. I am so glad he is pleased and satisfied with me.

"I have heard again from poor Ainslie. He had received the crushing news, and had borne it like a man; but his heart is cruelly torn; I think it will affect the whole tenor of his life. He is trying to act up to the full meaning of Mrs. Butler's

verses, and, what is more, to the full meaning of the New Testament.   For *her* sake,
and for his Saviour's sake, he strives to
' take hold of all high aims,' and to let his
light shine before men, *i.e.* the men of his
corps.   The subs., consequently, already
dub him a blue light, and shun walking
with him, for fear of what they call prosing.
They even almost send him to Coventry at
table, passing him over as if he were not
there.   This is what the corps he has left
would never have done ; it reduces him to
worse than solitude, because the *géne* of
their presence and bad talk cannot be
avoided ; but he says ' none of these things
move me.'   I'm sure I could not say as
much if I were in his place.   He is more
successful with the privates, and has found
it expedient to lay down total abstinence
as a foundation-stone ; nothing short of
it is effectual. He is always temperate,
therefore did not need the pledge himself,

but has taken it for the sake of example.
I know you'll admire this. *Aprópòs*, my
father's scheme includes water-drinking,
with grapes and raisins *ad libitum*. We
have very good vineyards, and also a
famous spring in the castle itself, and a
pseudo miraculous one at a shrine a little
way off, much resorted to by pilgrims.
He wants to start his sanatorium before
the grapes are gathered if he can. They
are very fine this season.

" Ever yours,
" Arthur Alured Ward."

It often happens to persons leading the
quietest of lives, that the affairs of their
intimate friends not only dovetail into, but
overlap each other; so that before one call
for sympathy is answered, another succeeds.
This gives perpetual movement and rich-
ness to their daily round, which to out-
siders, may appear as dull as the weed on

Lethe's wharf, but is not so. Those unconnected persons, especially if young, are often provokingly unconcerned in the welfare or success of each other, though all expect the first place in the interest of the common sympathizer, reminding one of the magazine contributor going up in a balloon with some of his coadjutors, who, when one of them fell out, said with hardly disguised triumph, " There's another serial gone !"

Thus while Miss Beaumorice's thoughts were pretty much engaged by Mary, and Margaret, and Alured, and Mrs. Caryl, she received a letter from Miss Partridge, undoubtingly claiming her corner. She said :

" How to apologize to you for my silence, my dear Miss Beaumorice, I know not," (Miss Beaumorice was ashamed not to have noticed that it *was* long) "but I will not waste paper on such an uninteresting subject. I write rather to tell you how specially pleased I was lately with a visit from Mr. Ward and his father. I cannot conceive how Dr. Ward could ever think such a visit necessary; but I enjoyed it too much to care to enquire too curiously whether it were called for or not. As he is an old friend of yours, I am sure it will gratify you to learn that I think him a charming man. What is more, the dowager countess thinks him so too; and she is a more competent judge. He quite took her fancy, and put her on so excellent a regimen that she is determined to give it a fair trial. We ranged over a variety of subjects, on all of which he spoke equally well; but what particularly delighted me was his scheme (so philanthropic!) of devoting that beautiful old castle of his to purposes of humanity, by making it a complete and most elegant sanatorium; reminding me greatly of what was done by the Count and Countess de Lagaraye. Poor Dr. Ward's Countess, unfortunately, is dead; yet, perhaps, that word must be used only in a limited sense; for, had she lived, this scheme would probably never have been thought of. You see, she was mistress of her own income, and there are half a dozen children to be provided for out of it. Dr. Ward is sole possessor of the castle, and the use he intends making of it argues a noble and self-devoting mind.

"I was glad to see Mr. Ward looking so well; and he seems to give his good father entire satisfaction. What a sad loss has his friend Mr. Ainslie sustained! I remember seeing him at your house in the spring; a dark, fine-looking young man, but I remember little of him beyond his personal appearance, being more engaged in conversing with Mr. Ward.

"The Countess is waiting for me to read to her, so I must conclude at once unless

I lose another post. Always, my dear Miss Beaumorice,

"Your affectionate friend,

"HENRIETTA PARTRIDGE.

"I *have* lost the post, but I will not say 'how tiresome!' for a momentous event impels me to write to you anew. I have used a strong word, but indeed, not too much so, for it concerns my whole future, the entire change of my mode of life. My dear friend, Dr. Ward has offered me his hand! I never was so utterly astounded. In the first place, our acquaintance is but of yesterday almost. He is even a greater stranger to me than it seems I am to him, for he says he has heard a good deal of me and feels he knows me completely, whereas I was hardly conscious of his existence. Then, my age, my want of fortune, of connexion, of attraction,—all, all overlooked by this generous man, so that I should feel quite overwhelmed, even were not the position he offers me so specially gratifying. I need hardly say in mere set phrase that I have accepted his offer. Have I done wrong? Does your heart tell you so? I no more thought of marriage than of being prime minister—certainly felt completely happy in the life Providence seemed to have allotted me; but now that a new, attractive sphere of happiness and usefulness opens before me, I hardly need counsel so much as congratulation.

" My dear friend, bear with this egotism —I want you to reassure me, to tell me you do not think me very silly; nay, more, that you think me a very happy woman. To be the mother of Alured! *That* will be one of my many privileges. The dear little orphaned children at the castle, too; it will be a privilege to train them and be tender to them. That office will be mine, probably, at no distant date, for Dr. Ward wishes to open the sanatorium speedily, and for me to be present at the opening. Lord and Lady Tilbury must be consulted about that: they have been so very kind to me that I cannot bear to put them to inconvenience. The Dowager Countess, happily for me, is my fast friend, and promises her influence with them, so that no serious obstacle threatens to arise. My head is so over-full that it is a good thing there is not an inch of paper left even for crossing. Farewell ! my dear friend."

Miss Beaumorice's first impulse was to laugh heartily at this strange *dénouement ;* but people, when alone, seldom laugh loud or long ; which shows what a conventional thing laughter is. But she was highly diverted, and also extremely pleased. Such an excellent thing for Miss Partridge ! for them both, in fact, though at first it struck her that it was a great come-down for Dr. Ward—that he might, in a worldly sense, have done much better for himself. What a good thing, then, that he did *not* take a worldly part—that he valued sense and sweet temper, and the many good qualities Miss Partridge undoubtedly possessed, more than the position and wealth which were not hers. It was certainly a wise choice, for she was completely qualified to be the female head of the sanatorium, whereas many would neither have been equal to it nor have felt it a compliment to be supposed so. Altogether, she thought it a most eligible engagement ; and as she wrote to Miss Partridge to tell her so, her cheerful thoughts succeeded one another

"Fast as the periods from her flowing quill,"

till she completed a letter straight from the heart that went to the heart, and made Miss Partridge resolve to keep it all her life. Nor could she withhold it from Dr. Ward, who was extremely desirous to know how Miss Beaumorice would write on the subject; and the result was that instead of feeling a rejected suitor and undervalued man, he was confirmed in the character of her fast friend.

Miss Beaumorice longed to know what Alured would think of it. He did not leave her long in doubt. He wrote delightedly, thought his father's happiness secured, and rejoiced in the prospect of so attachable a mother-in-law. He ended by exclaiming, "What a nice thing for Idalia!"

Perhaps Lord and Lady Tilbury might occasion obstacles after all. But no; by a fortunate series of events, they were rendered highly pleased to have an opportunity of engaging a German fräulein of first-rate abilities, whom, if it had not been painful to shelve poor Miss Partridge, they would have been glad to secure at any price. This found its way to the Dowager Countess, who told them by return of post of Miss Partridge's eligible engagement;

so that nothing hindered from expediting the marriage as soon as possible; Lord Tilbury crowning all by promising to give her away.

If anything were needed to overcome any lingering delays, it was found in old Lady Tilbury's deciding that she should like to visit her *protegée* before the sanatorium was opened, that she might make proof on the spot of its beneficial arrangements. All, then, went merry as a marriage bell, and Miss Beaumorice soon had the satisfaction of learning from letters and newspapers that the wedding had taken place.

Meanwhile the Brookes did not start without her going to Longfield for the express purpose of hearing Mr. Brooke's last sermon. To her great pleasure, it was much better and heartier than his first.

"What was it made the difference in your preaching, this evening?" said she, as she walked home with him and Margaret in the dusk, for the days were now shortening.

"Did you perceive it?" said he, smiling. "These people I am going to have been accustomed to extempore preaching; and Dr. Garrow told me, if I would win their good graces, I should preach extempore also; so I have made several experiments at our cottage lectures and find I like it, and that others like it too."

"I am so glad! I can carry home the greater part of what you said, which was not the case before."

"Well, I fancy it is the right way, when one has some degree of readiness. Of course that increases with practice. Dr. Garrow used always to read his sermons, but since his sight has somewhat failed, he chiefly preaches extempore, and I own I find his sermons ten times better."

She drank tea with them for the last

time, and remained till quite dark. Then
Mr. Brooke and Margaret accompanied her
to her own gate by the light of the harvest
moon. Mary begged her not to think of
seeing them off in the morning, but she
said she should certainly try for a last look
and word at the station; and she had it,
too. The last words were most affectionate,
the last looks cheerful; and though older
heads are often troubled with forebodings,
Miss Beaumorice would not indulge in
them, but only entrust them, in hearty
faith, to their heavenly Father's guidance.
She knew that—

> "All common things, each day's events,
> That with the hour begin and end,
> Our pleasures and our discontents,
> Are rounds by which we may ascend."

She was sensible of a little loneliness
when she re-entered her house, and immediately addressed herself to the duty that
came nearest, and wrote to her uncle

George, who for some years had always spent his birthday with her. She asked him if he could not extend his holiday a little, and come to her overnight; it would give her very great pleasure.

Then she called on Mrs. Caryl, who was poring over a letter from her niece Edith, proposing all sorts of impossible things, with only a dim idea how ill she had been. She wished Mrs. Caryl could winter with them, she was sure it would do her so much good, and added, that they were now so much nearer England, that if her aunt could but manage to cross the channel, she herself would await her landing, and take good care of her from that moment.

"It is too bright and pleasant to think of," said Mrs. Caryl, regretfully, as she laid the letter aside.

"Why should not you?" said Miss Beaumorice; "your book is off your hands. Do you mind the expense?"

"No; my kind publishers have told me I may have my copyright money whenever I like."

"Why should you not go, then?" said Miss Beaumorice.

"My dear friend, I am not so young as I have been, nor as you are now.   If Edith could have come quite over, I think I could have implicitly put myself into her care, but I know she cannot."

"Would you accept of me in her place?"

"Do you really mean it?   Oh, I am sure you cannot!"

"What should hinder me?   I think I should like it very much.   Just let me tide over my uncle's birthday, which he always spends with me."

"To be sure I will," said Mrs. Caryl, with delight.   "I, too, shall have arrangements to make, but I will not trouble myself with many.   Just turn the key on my papers, and let Hester have her mother with her till I come back. Why, you make me feel quite young again. I can trust everything to your management. Our journey together will be an absolute treat."

CHAPTER XIII.

GLIDING DOWN.

" May I, with look ungloomed by guile,
And wearing virtue's livery, smile,
Prone the distressed to relieve,
And little trespasses forgive ;
With income not a fortune's power,
And skill to make a busy hour
With trips to town, life to amuse,
To purchase books and hear the news."

GREEN.

MISS BEAUMORICE made this offer quite on the spur of the moment. She had not seen the sea for some years, and had never crossed it alone in her life, so that her undertaking the charge of Mrs. Caryl had something amusing in it. At all events it put her and her household in excellent spirits ; even the maids thought they had a share in it, and were sure she would have many entertaining things to recount when she came back.

And now ensued porings over Bradshaw, and setting things generally to rights, preparatory to the mighty journey. The Nunehams took lively interest in it, and were continually bringing messages and offering services. The weather was warm, ripe, and genial, without any change of colour yet in the foliage, except that the Virginian creepers were beginning to turn scarlet, and the horse - chestnuts auburn, and the walnuts russet. There was only the ghost of a fog in the morning.

Their destination was Dinan, where Mrs. Caryl's brother now awaited her at the boarding-house of the popular Mrs. Barr. Edith Caryl would receive her aunt at St.

Malo; there would be no need for Miss Beaumorice even to land unless she liked it. But Miss Beaumorice thought that if she went so far on her friend's account, she would at least take a look at Dinan on her own. Meanwhile she provided for the safety and comfort of her servants in her short absence, and made ready for her uncle on the eve of his birthday.

He was a kindly, amiable old man, reminding her of her father in many ways. They had always been fond of one another, and now she was his only near relative in England, though he had a married son settled in Brazil.

The meeting was very cordial and pleasant; he seemed strengthened and freshened by the country air, and talked of walking before breakfast, and riding a safe horse after it.

"It was a good thought of yours, my dear," said he, "to propose my coming to-day. It gives me two nights of country air, and I am sure my lungs will thank you for it."

"My dear uncle, I am only sorry this should be the first time. I had no idea you would like to come to me."

"Like it ? Why, you are the only one now, to remind me of your father ! My dear, I was always fond of you, and fond of the country."

"I wish you could be persuaded to live in the country entirely, uncle ; somewhere near me."

"It takes a good deal of persuasion to get a business man out of his regular groove. But I have always meant to re-tire some time or other ; and it must be soon too, or my business may retire from me."

He was silent a little, and then said, "My head is not what it was ; and my strength is not what it was. But I think

I might last out a little longer if I became a sleeping partner, and had a snug little box somewhere."

"Let me look about for one. May I ?"

"Well, you may look out, but I don't say I'll take it : so don't go too far. When it comes to the point, I might not be equal to it. By-the-bye, poor Tomkinson had a stroke the other day. He's ten years older than me, poor fellow."

"Uncle, I seriously wish you would think of retiring, and leave the business to younger men. I am sure you might if you would."

"Oh, I have more to retire on than I should want. Henry is doing well now."

"Do, then ! Take the ease you so well have earned. I should enjoy having you for my neighbour."

"It is a pleasant notion," said he, smiling.

" And you could have a season ticket and run up to town whenever you wished, and have old friends from town whenever you liked."

" You make it out very pleasantly. I generally give myself a week at Ramsgate or Margate in the autumn, but last year I felt alone in a crowd, so I thought I would not go again."

" You would not feel alone here. There are some very nice people."

" Oh, I should not want many. When I know there is some one to whom I can speak a word, I get on very well without speaking it."

Then they talked of old times, and of recent events ; and afterwards had three games of chess ; and she had a fire, and he asked, " Was it not a shame ?" and yet enjoyed it. He confessed to liking arrowroot with a little brandy in it for supper ; and Alice made it exactly to his liking. When Miss Beaumorice had read the evening chapter and prayers, he said,—

" My dear, how much your voice resembles your mother's! I have not heard a chapter read so much to my mind, I don't know when. I feel inclined to say with the Queen of Sheba, 'Happy are thy servants!' By-the-bye, where did you contrive to pick up a couple of such winsome lasses? If I have that little box we were speaking of, I suppose I must have a couple of lasses too. But what would poor old Mrs. Brown do? and where could she go? I suppose I should have to pension her off."

" Perhaps the successor to your chambers might like to take Mrs. Brown too."

" That is possible; that is a good idea. To tell you the truth, I am not very fond of Mrs. Brown. She humours, tries to manage me ; and I am not fond of either. I like to manage my servants ; not to be managed by them. My love, I believe this is your time for shutting up. My own time too, when I don't have a nap ; and I have not felt the least drowsy this evening. Let me be called early, please; good-night, my dear, God bless you."

It gave her pleasure to receive his blessing.

She did not expect him to be ready for breakfast quite at her usual time ; but, happening to look from her bedroom window, she saw him walking round the garden quite alertly, stopping now and then to examine a flower. When he joined her at breakfast, he said, complacently, " I have cut off about thirty dead roses with my nail scissors. There are many things I could find to do in a garden such as yours. Did you lay it out yourself ?"

"Yes, with a ball of twine; and then the gardener cut out the borders under my direction. It was only a piece of inclosed field when I came here."

"The planting must have cost you a pretty penny."

"Well, I saved in other things—bought fewer dresses."

"Well done. And your rent is—"

"Fifty pounds. Taxes fifteen."

"And you have—"

"Four bedrooms and two dressing-rooms."

"And enough too," said he, decidedly. "Enough in all conscience. Are you ever—afraid of thieves?"

Miss Beaumorice laughed, and said she was not.

"But yet you have no man in the house."

"I don't think that much signifies."

"Not even a dog."

" I don't think I want one."

" What should you do if you were frightened ?"

" I might ring a large dinner-bell."

" Certainly you might, if you have one," said her uncle, quite satisfied.

She did not tell him that if she rang it, probably no one would hear or answer it.

After breakfast, his thoughts still turning on a safe horse, Miss Beaumorice, knowing of a very old and steady one belonging to a retired tradesman, proposed their going to look after it. On the way Mr. Beaumorice observed the church, and asked if there would be a service that morning, to which she replied in the affirmative.

" Well, then," said he, " I should like to go if you are going. I am not a ritualist by any means, and, if I were, should find it difficult in town to get to church on week-days ; but in the country it is different, and I always like to improve my opportunities. So, you know, I can put off my ride till the afternoon."

In one way and another, the day passed very happily ; including a chat with Mr. Nuneham, a cheerful greeting from Mr. Finch, a jog-trot round the common, and a nap over the newspaper. In the evening, Mr. Beaumorice asked his niece if she could remember any of her old songs.

"Oh, uncle !" said she, laughing, " I have lost my G !"

She played him several chants, however ; and afterwards, chat, chess, and reading filled up the evening. They parted with great affection the next morning; she begging him to pay her a longer visit in the winter, which he promised to think about.

Next came the mighty journey, which amused no one more than Mr. Finch, who looked upon it as quite remarkable, but gave it his entire approval.

"I only hope," said he, "there will be no equinoctial gales."

"I hope a good deal more than that," said Miss Beaumorice.

To her great thankfulness, Mrs. Caryl bore well the journey to Southampton and the fourteen hours' voyage to Jersey. There the unprotected females landed at half-past two in the afternoon, went to bed for a few hours, and dined in their own room, though there was a *table d'hôte.* Mrs. Caryl passed the first half of the next day in bed, which gave Miss Beaumorice the opportunity of strolling through the quaint little town of St. Helier's. Thirty people or more were going to make an omnibus excursion round the island the next morning; but she did not wish to join them. She preferred an evening of quiet and amusing chat with Mrs. Caryl, and another walk in the morning; after which they started in the afternoon for St. Malo.

The little voyage was short and prosperous. A sweet-looking young lady, with whom Miss Beaumorice at once felt *en rapport*, was in waiting for them with a hired carriage which was to take them to Dinan. She welcomed her aunt most affectionately, and warmly pressed Miss Beaumorice to stay with them as long as she could. It proved that the boarding-house was over-full at present; Mrs. Caryl would have to share Edith's room; but if Miss Beaumorice did not mind sleeping under another roof, there was one close at hand, belonging to a native bourgeois family, where she could be as comfortable as possible.

Miss Beaumorice immediately said that she should much prefer this, it would be so fresh and *piquant*, and Mrs. Caryl who had changed countenance when she heard of the noisy influx of strangers at Mrs. Barr's, thought the bourgeois domicile would be much quieter and more suitable for her; which she was confirmed in when Edith said the occupant was "une vieux demoiselle," as the old chroniclers say, courteous and kindly and simple-minded as possible, with a companion of about her own age, and an old physician of eighty, who had lived with them fifteen years.

Edith spoke rather regretfully of the disappointment it would be not to have them under the same roof; but her father and she had mutually decided that it was extremely likely Mrs. Caryl would prefer the quieter abode. And thus it came to pass that, arriving at Dinan, they went direct to the house in question, modest enough in pretension, but where the courtesy and cleanliness would have made up for much greater deficiencies, and where a good-sized, pretty bedroom, partly fitted up as a sitting-room, exactly suited for Mrs. Caryl, adjoined a smaller room that would equally well suit Miss Beaumorice.

Here, then, they made themselves as comfortable as need be; Mr. Caryl paid his sister a short but very affectionate visit, and went away, hoping to see much more of her when she had recovered from the fatigue of her journey.

In the morning, the cheerful-looking Breton maid brought them coffee and toast in their own rooms. Mrs. Caryl was fatigued enough to remain in bed till late in the afternoon, but Miss Beaumorice was glad to start on a visit she had much at heart, to the Château of La Garage.

With her head full of Mrs. Norton's poems and Cathenos' prose narrative, hardly less romantic, she was sorry to find the hospice now occupied by cows and pigs; while the château, once a glorious old mansion, was crumbling into ruin. Only the front and a portion of a beautiful tower, choked with weeds, remained. Miss Beaumorice thought of the time when sick people, far and near, flocked to the spot for medical attendance and benevolent aid; and as she strayed onwards, through woods and green lanes, her thoughts reverted to Dr. Ward's sanatorium; but there was this difference between them, that whereas La Garage was entirely gratuitous, the off-spring of a charity that sought for no earthly reward, Dr. Ward intended his to bring a considerable pecuniary return; it was, in fact, a speculation.

Miss Beaumorice found her way back in time for the eleven o'clock *déjeûner* of buttered eggs, cold meat, and cider, which lasted the family till the five o'clock dinner. In the afternoon Edith, who had spent the morning with her aunt, volunteered to accompany Miss Beaumorice to the little village of Thadin, where the tombs of the Count and Countess de La Garage might yet be seen, and where poor women still resorted to offer prayer.

Thenceforth every day brought its quiet pleasures; and though Mrs. Caryl did not immediately recover from her journey, Miss Beaumorice had the satisfaction of leaving her tolerably well and very happy at the week's end. Before she left Dinan, she had the pleasure of witnessing the annual fêtes there, when the mountain slopes were garlanded with coloured lamps and Chinese lanterns, and hundreds of young peasants danced to the music of an excellent military band. The scene was so un-English that it made a strong impression on her, and was long remembered afterwards; but a little of such variety suited her better than a great deal, and she gladly returned to her quiet home, refreshed and enlivened by her brief holiday.

Cheerful letters from Mary, Margaret, and Alured awaited her return. Her uncle too, wrote heartily, said his son talked of coming over in the spring, and that he felt much inclined to spend the winter near her.

Then up and spake Miss Beaumorice in the warmth of her heart, and proposed that he should be her guest for the winter, and promised to make him as comfortable as she possibly could. The readiness with which this invitation was accepted proved how much pleasure it gave, and evinced that he now, in his declining years, felt the need of " the soft pillow of a woman's mind." Thenceforth he wrote to her every week, anticipating the approach of Christmas with almost a schoolboy's zest. Her heart drew towards him with great tenderness ; to be still dear to some, still useful to some, had long been her wish, and she had it.

Short as her absence had been, it had

brought to a climax an incipient attachment between Jessy and a good young car-
penter. Miss Beaumorice heard of their
engagement with lively interest, promised
Jessy a present of house linen, and bought
it in good time that it might be an evening
amusement to her to make it up. How
should she fill her place ? Why, the aunt
who had spent a week in the house during
Miss Beaumorice's absence, had a daughter
of sixteen, who would thankfully step into
it if Miss Beaumorice would not mind the
usual training. Certainly not ; she would
gladly make trial of her, and with Alice's
superintendence there was no doubt of her
doing well.

Thus instead of looking forward to a
lonely, inactive winter, she was as cheerful
in her way as Miss Partridge—pooh—Mrs.
Ward was in hers. Lively accounts came
over from the Schloss, and everything
seemed prospering and promising ; but Miss

Beaumorice never wavered in her preference for her own life, nor had a shadow of envy or regret.

Mrs. Caryl's letters were delightful. Her intercourse with her brother seemed to rejuvenize her; the air and scenery suited her; her book came out and was a success. Miss Beaumorice had the pleasure of seeing it well reviewed; and of forwarding the notices to her. But before *they* came out, the reading public to whom she always conscientiously gave of her best, whether that were up to the mark or under it, pronounced its approving verdict, and a new edition was called for at Christmas.

Miss Beaumorice thought "Where is the sting, now, of the unkind words that hurt her so much in the spring? What but their medicinal influence on her mind, stringing it up to bring forth good thoughts even in her pain that may cheer and benefit others? As long as she can do this, she does not live in vain.   But in fact, she will always do this, now, living or dead, while her healthful words remain in print.   This seems to me an authoress's best aim.   Do I desire to be one?   I think persistent effort is not in me; but I know, now, the way to begin, if the desire should seize me."

When Miss Beaumorice came to " add up " her expenses at the year's end, she set down in black and white what she had already certified herself of, that she was on the right side of the post!   How was this?   She had had no legacies, no lucky investments : there had been no niggardliness, no painful abridgement of charities. It must have been from the blessing of God on sheer good-management and self denial, industry and economy, and " the geometrical distribution of expenses !"

We may as well leave Miss Beaumorice at this point.   Young people under twenty are apt to think the interest of life must be pretty well over at thirty—certainly at forty—indubitably so at fifty! What a splendid mistake!

THE END.

BILLING, PRINTER, GUILDFORD, SURREY.